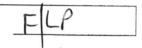

THE LAREDO GANG

Ex-deputy US marshal Jack Tracy returns to the Box T Ranch in Colorado and discovers that his family has been murdered by the Laredo gang. Starting out on a lonely and perilous journey to bring the gang to justice, he is joined by Ruth Mailer whose father was also murdered by the outlaws. But they are risking death as they ride through the Texas Panhandle and the Indian Territory. Will they survive long enough to complete their task?

ALAN IRWIN

THE LAREDO GANG

Complete and Unabridged

LINFORD
Leicester

First published in Great Britain in 2007 by
Robert Hale Limited
London

First Linford Edition
published 2008
by arrangement with
Robert Hale Limited
London

British Library CIP Data

Irwin, Alan, *1916 –*
    The Laredo gang.—Large print ed.—
Linford western library
1. Western stories
2. Large type books
I. Title
823.9'14 [F]

ISBN 978–1–84782–206–2

Published by
F. A. Thorpe (Publishing)
Anstey, Leicestershire

Set by Words & Graphics Ltd.
Anstey, Leicestershire
Printed and bound in Great Britain by
T. J. International Ltd., Padstow, Cornwall

This book is printed on acid-free paper

1

Jack Tracy rode to the top of the rise and paused for a while to look ahead, to the south, at the Box T ranch house and the other buildings standing nearby. The ranch stood south of Pueblo, in Colorado.

Then, as Jack looked beyond the buildings, he caught sight of four riders, in the far distance, heading south. As he watched they disappeared from view.

Six years earlier, at the age of twenty, Jack had left the Box T. His parents Joe and Martha, and his brother Billy, had been sad to see him go, but Jack had a strong desire to explore Texas, Kansas and the Indian Territory.

Over the past six years he had achieved this ambition, working as a ranch hand, trail hand, and finally, for the past eighteen months, as a deputy US marshal in the Indian Territory.

During this time he had gained a reputation as a fearless and competent lawman.

Then a letter arrived from his mother, telling him his father had not been well for a while. There was no specific request for him to return to the Box T, but reading between the lines Jack sensed that she was deeply worried and would welcome his return. He decided to leave for Colorado, in the knowledge that his job would be waiting for him if he returned.

He started riding towards the Box T ranch house. He was a broad-shouldered man, around five feet ten tall, still sitting easily in the saddle despite the many miles he had covered that day. He had a pleasant face, topped by a mop of unruly dark hair showing under the brim of his tall Texas hat.

As he neared the house he came upon four horses standing in a listless manner, with their heads down. As one of them moved he could see that it was lame. Pausing to look them over, he could see that they bore all the signs of having been ridden hard and long, almost to the limit of their endurance.

As he looked towards the buildings he could see no signs of life. Suddenly he had a premonition that all was not well. He rode up to the house and dismounted. The door was ajar. He pushed it open and walked inside, calling out as he did so. There was no response. He found nobody in the living-room or kitchen. In the kitchen there was a piece of bloodstained cloth lying on the floor, close to several large spots of blood. On a table was a bowl of bloodstained water, and the remains of a roll of bandage. It seemed clear that a wound had been treated there recently.

He went upstairs, where the three bedrooms were located, and went into the first room along the passage. He pulled up short as he stepped inside. His father was lying on the bed in his night clothing. There was a bullet hole in the centre of his forehead. His mother, fully dressed, was lying on her back across the bed, with a sixgun by her side. As he walked up to her Jack could see that she had been shot in the chest. She was not breathing.

Badly shocked, Jack stood looking down at his parents for a few moments. Then he looked in the other two bedrooms. His brother Billy was in neither of them. He left the house and ran over to the bunkhouse. There was nobody inside. He ran over to the barn and pushed the heavy door open.

Billy and Turner, one of his father's hands, lay side by side on the floor. Turner had been shot once in the chest, Billy twice. Both were dead. Stunned by the discovery of the four bodies, including three members of his own family, Jack left the barn and walked towards the house.

Before he reached it he caught sight of two riders approaching from the east. He stopped near the house and stood awaiting their arrival. As they passed the four horses which Jack had seen earlier they paused to look them over, before riding on again towards Jack.

As they drew closer Jack recognized them as Rod Bailey, foreman of the Box T and a close friend of the Tracys, accompanied by Barclay, one of the ranch hands. A moment later they recognized Jack. They rode up to him and dismounted.

'Jack!' said Bailey, 'it's great to see you again.'

He walked up to Jack and shook his hand vigorously. But his smile faded as he saw the look on Jack's face.

'What's wrong Jack?' he asked.

'I've only just got here, Rod,' said Jack, 'and I'm finding it hard to take in what's happened. Ma and Pa and Billy have all been shot dead. And Turner as well. I don't know who did it, but maybe those four tired horses over there have something to do with it. As I was riding in I saw four riders, a long way to the south, just before they passed out of view.'

Deeply shocked, the foreman and

Barclay followed Jack to the bedroom, then the barn.

When they left the barn Jack asked Bailey if there was still a sheriff's office in Pueblo.

'There is,' Bailey replied, 'and Nolan is still doing the job. I reckon you remember him?'

'I do,' said Jack. 'The two of us were pretty friendly. We'd better get him out here. And the undertaker too.'

Bailey told Barclay to ride to Pueblo for Sheriff Nolan and an undertaker. When the ranch hand had departed, Jack and the foreman closely examined the bedroom and barn, where the murders had taken place, to see if there were any indications as to who had committed the crimes. But their search was fruitless.

They went to look at the horses in the pasture, and Bailey noticed that four were missing. Then they inspected the ground surrounding the ranch buildings. The picture which eventually emerged was that of four men riding in from the north on horses which were on the point of exhaustion. The men had surprised Billy and Turner in the barn, had killed them, and had then gone to the house, where they had killed Jack's parents and had attended to a wounded man in the kitchen. Then they had taken four horses from the pasture, and had transferred their own saddles and bridles to these before riding off to the south.

Jack and Bailey went into the house, where the foreman explained that Jack's father had been laid up for a spell with heart trouble, but had recently appeared to be well on the way to recovery.

County Sheriff Nolan arrived with Barclay two hours later. Nolan, a rangy, middle-aged man wearing a neat black moustache had proved over the years to be a conscientious and capable lawman. As he followed Jack into the bedroom, then the barn, sensing the anguish of his old friend, his anger mounted. Jack told him about his sighting, from the top of the ridge, of four riders heading south, and gave his opinion on what had happened on the Box T just before his arrival.

'I think you've got it right, Jack,' said the sheriff, 'and I think that the reason for them killing everybody here was to give them time to get well away before the alarm was raised. But they must be a real cold-blooded lot. All they needed to do was tie them up good and tight.'

'It could be,' said Jack, 'that they didn't want anybody passing their descriptions on to the law.'

'Just now,' said Nolan, 'my deputy is out with a posse, chasing some rustlers, and I don't know when they'll be back. I'm going to go after those killers myself, while their tracks are still fresh. If I write a message for my deputy telling him to follow me with a posse as soon as he can, will you get somebody to take it to Pueblo?'

'Rod'll see to that,' said Jack, 'but you're not going alone. I'm going with you.'

He turned to the foreman.

'I've got to go, Rod,' he said. 'Those men have got to be caught. I'm not sure when I'll be back, but if I don't make it for the funeral, I know that you'll see them all buried right, and I'd be obliged if you'd look after the Box T for the time being. Hire some help if you need it.'

'Sure,' said the foreman. 'I'll take care of everything here till you get back. And I'll make sure the sheriff's message gets to Pueblo.'

Fifteen minutes later Jack and the sheriff left, after getting a description of the stolen horses from Bailey. They headed for the point where the four riders had disappeared from Jack's view. They picked up the fresh horse tracks and followed them south.

Three hours later, without any sighting of their quarry, they paused as they came near to a low ridge which ran across their path. The tracks were heading towards a gap in the ridge.

'I reckon we ain't all that far behind

them,' said Jack, 'probably a whole lot closer than they're expecting anyone to be. Come dark, if they decide to make camp and take a rest, maybe we'll be able to sneak up on them.'

'I figure you're right,' said Nolan, and they rode on towards the gap. As they entered it they could see that it was bordered by steep rocky slopes, while the floor was littered with large boulders. Feeling a premonition of danger, Jack reined in his mount. The sheriff followed suit. Jack's premonition of danger became stronger.

'It's just struck me,' he said, 'that maybe those four took it into their heads to have one man watch the back trail for a while to check whether they were being followed. If I'm right, I can't think of a better place for an ambush than this.'

'You're right,' said Nolan. 'We'd better find another way to the far side of this ridge.'

But they were too late. Before they could turn their mounts, a hidden rifleman at the top of the slope fired two shots in their direction. The first shot hit Nolan in the chest. He fell from his horse and was dead before he hit the ground. The second shot struck Jack in the side as he threw himself out of the saddle, pulling his rifle from the saddle holster as he did so. On hitting the ground he ran desperately towards a large boulder nearby. As he was taking shelter behind it a third shot, narrowly missing him, ricocheted from the surface of the boulder.

Jack was now well protected from further fire, and he was able to watch out for any movement at the top of the slope. As he stood there, he heard two rifle shots, with a one-minute interval between them. There was no indication that the shots had been aimed at him. He peered around the side of the boulder, along the floor of the pass. Nolan was still lying on the ground. Beyond him the two horses they had been riding were lying motionless.

There was no further fire and after a

while Jack began to suspect that the rifleman had left. But he could not be sure. He decided to stay where he was until nightfall, which was near. While watching and listening for any movements nearby, he checked the wound in his side. The bullet had hit the left side of his upper chest and was lodged inside. The wound was bleeding profusely. He made a pad with his bandanna and held it over the wound in an attempt to stanch the flow of blood.

When at last darkness fell, Jack left the shelter of the boulder and walked over to the sheriff. He confirmed that Nolan was dead. He walked on to the horses and confirmed that they also were dead, with gunshot wounds in the heads. It was clear that the man who had fired the shots was an expert marksman.

From his horse Jack took a large water-bottle and a roll of bandage which were in the saddlebag. Then he returned to the body of the sheriff.

Slowly and painfully, working in the dark, he covered the body with some of the small pieces of rock that littered the ground. When he had finished the job he lay down near the boulder, exhausted, and rested for a while.

When he had recovered a little, he cleaned his wound with water as best he could, then made a fresh pad and held it in place with a length of bandage around his chest. When he was satisfied that the bandage was reasonably secure he walked out of the pass and back along the trail which he and Nolan had followed earlier.

He trudged slowly along through the darkness, keeping one hand pressed over the pad covering the wound on his chest. He could feel his strength slowly ebbing away, and it was only a grim determination to bring justice to the killers who had struck once again that kept him going. But just before dawn his legs refused to function any longer and he collapsed on to the ground. He was still conscious and made several failed attempts to rise to his feet, before lying motionless on the ground.

The posse came across him three hours later. It was a posse of five men, led by Deputy Sheriff John Barker, who was known to Jack. Deeply shocked, they listened as Jack told them about the ambush, and described the exact location of Nolan's body.

'About half an hour back,' Barker told Jack, 'we passed about a mile east of some ranch buildings. D'you reckon you could make it there riding double?'

'I reckon so,' said Jack.

Barker spoke to Pendry, one of the men riding with him.

'Take Tracy to the ranch,' he said, 'and ask them to get a doctor to see him. I think there's a doctor in a small town not far from there. Then come after us. We'll be following the one who killed the sheriff. We'll arrange later to get his body to Pueblo.'

When Jack arrived with Pendry at the Circle Dot ranch house he was on the verge of collapse, hardly able to maintain his seat on the horse. Pendry dismounted, helped Jack down, and held him upright.

The door of the ranch house opened and rancher Ed Spencer walked out, closely followed by his wife Jane. Spencer was a stocky, bearded man in his forties. He walked over and helped Pendry support Jack.

'I'm from a posse that's chasing a gang of killers,' said Pendry. 'Mr Tracy here's been wounded. Will you tend him and get a doctor to see him? Myself, I aim to catch up with the posse.'

'Sure,' replied Spencer. 'We'll do what we can, and glad to. There's a doctor in Lanry. I'll ride there for him right now.'

Pendry and the rancher helped Jack into the house and sat him on a chair. Then Pendry rode off, and Spencer, whose hands were out on the range, saddled a horse and left for Lanry, a small town a few miles to the west. Meanwhile, the rancher's wife, a slim, pleasant woman, tended to Jack's wound pending the doctor's arrival.

A little under two hours later Spencer returned with Doc Sherman, who examined Jack, extracted the bullet, and cleaned and bandaged the wound.

'You were lucky,' he said to Jack. 'If that bullet had gone in a little lower and to one side you'd have died on the spot. As it is, if there's no infection, you should be fit to ride back to your ranch in a couple of weeks. I'll call in here now and again to see how you're getting on.'

Jack looked at Jane Spencer.

'You're welcome to stay with us just as long as it takes,' she said.

★ ★ ★

Four days later Deputy Sheriff Barker rode in from the south with his posse. They were leading four saddled horses. Barker went inside the house to see Jack.

He told Jack that the posse had

followed the tracks of the four horses to a point about sixty miles south of the Circle Dot, when they came upon four saddled horses grazing in a grassy hollow. There was no sign of the riders and no indication of where they might have gone.

'The four horses we found,' said Barker, 'tally with the descriptions of the ones stolen from the Box T. We have them with us. We searched all around the area but we couldn't find any sign of the riders of the horses. And we couldn't find anybody who'd seen them. So we had to give up the chase. If you like, we'll drop off three of the horses at the Box T and leave one here for you to ride back on.'

'Thanks,' said Jack. 'I aim to ride back to the Box T just as soon as I can. Tell Rod Bailey I'll be turning up there in a week or so.'

Seven days later Jack thanked the Spencers for their help and headed for the Box T.

When he reached the ranch he told

Bailey and Barclay that he would shortly be resuming his search for the killers of his family and Turner. He asked the foreman to continue to run the ranch.

'I'll do it, and glad to,' said Bailey. 'I guess you know what a dangerous job it is that you're taking on. When are you aiming to leave?'

'After I've had a talk with Deputy Sheriff Barker,' Jack replied. 'I'll ride to Pueblo in the morning.'

'There'll be no need for that,' said Bailey, who was looking out of the window. 'I see him riding up to the house.'

Jack went out and invited Barker inside.

'I figured you'd be back by now,' said the deputy. 'I've got some news about the men you and the sheriff were following. It seems pretty certain that it was the Laredo gang.'

Jack had heard of the notorious Laredo gang. During bank and stage-coach robberies they invariably kept their faces well covered. But there was one distinguishing feature about the gang. During the course of a robbery, apart from a few shouted commands to the people they were confronting, the gang worked in silence, except that the leader invariably hummed the tune of the popular and plaintive cowboy lament 'The Streets of Laredo'. This was possibly intended to calm the nerves of the gang. Since the identity of the leader of the gang was not known to the law or the general public, the gang came to be known as the Laredo gang.

'We first heard of the gang a year ago,' said Barker, 'when they robbed a stagecoach in Wyoming. Since then they've pulled off a bank robbery in Colorado and a stagecoach robbery in the Texas Panhandle. They've left a trail of dead lawmen and citizens behind them. Up to now we've no idea of who they are or where they might be hiding out between jobs. Most likely that would be in the

19

Indian Territory, I reckon.

'It turns out that three days before your folks were killed, the gang robbed a bank in Cheyenne. One of them was hit by a rifle bullet, but they rode over the border into Colorado before the posse could catch up with them. The sheriff in Wyoming tried to telegraph Sheriff Nolan to tell him they had crossed the border, but the telegraph line was down.'

'I aim to go after them,' said Jack, 'but it seems I ain't got a lot to go on. I think I'll ride to the place where you found those four horses. If I spend some time around there maybe I can find out how they managed to disappear like that.'

'D'you reckon,' asked Barker, 'that the man who shot the sheriff would recognize you again?'

'If he saw me again, I don't think he would,' Jack replied. 'He wasn't that close and he was firing down on us. And I didn't waste no time getting behind that boulder.'

'I'm wishing you luck,' said the deputy before riding off. 'If you manage to locate the gang anywhere in this county, we'll give you any help we can.'

3399401

F|LP

2

Jack left the Box T the following morning, after making all the necessary arrangements for Bailey to run the ranch during his absence. He headed for the place described to him by Barker, where the four Box T horses had been found.

He was still fifteen miles from his destination when he saw ahead of him the buildings of a homestead. He rode towards them, intending to enquire whether anyone there had seen the four riders he was seeking. As he neared the house he saw two saddled horses tied to a hitching-rail outside. There was no one in sight around the buildings.

He dismounted and tied his horse to the rail, then walked up to the door. As he raised a hand to knock on it he heard the shrill sound of a woman's scream coming from inside the house.

The sound ceased abruptly, but was repeated a moment later. Then there was silence. Holding his sixgun, Jack opened the door and stepped quietly inside. Quickly he checked that there was nobody downstairs. Then he silently mounted the stairs. As he reached the top he heard another scream coming from the bedroom. He went up to the door, which was slightly ajar, pushed hard on it, and stepped inside the room.

A woman was lying on the bed. A big man was bending down over her with his hands around her throat. A second man, slimmer and shorter than his companion, was standing with his back to Jack, watching the assault on the woman. Both men were roughly dressed and each of them was wearing a gun in a right-hand holster.

Seeing Jack, the big man released his hold on the woman. Shouting a warning to his partner, he stood up, drawing his gun and turning to face the man in the doorway. Choosing his target on the body, Jack sent a bullet into the big man's upper right arm, and his gun fell to the floor before it had been fired.

The same fate befell the short man. Too slow to beat the second shot from Jack's Peacemaker, he was shot in almost exactly the same place as his partner and he lost his hold on his gun. Keeping the two men covered, Jack picked up the two guns and laid them on the bed. He ordered the two men to lie face down on the floor well away from the bed.

'Let's be quick about it,' he said, 'unless you want a bullet in the other arm as well.'

When the two men had done as Jack ordered he turned to look at the woman. Badly shocked, she was sitting up on the bed gulping air into her lungs, and fingering a large bruise on her face. She was a slim, attractive woman in her twenties.

'You all right?' asked Jack.

'Apart from this bruise I'm all right

now,' she replied, 'but I reckon you showed up just in time. I was on my own here when these two rode up. My husband's in town. He'll be back here before long.'

'D'you know these men?' asked Jack.

'Never seen them before,' she replied. 'They forced their way into the house and made me fix a meal for them. Then they searched downstairs for money and when they couldn't find any they dragged me up here and searched the bedroom. But they found none here either. When you turned up they were trying to find out from me whether we had some money hidden away somewhere.'

'I'll wait here till your husband gets back,' said Jack, 'then we can decide what to do with these two. They ain't hurt that bad. I'll take them into the barn and tie them up tight if you'll hold a gun on them while I do it. Then we'll come back here.'

'I'll be glad to,' she said.

When they returned to the house,

leaving the two men securely tied up in the barn, the woman told Jack that her name was Jane Farren, and that she and her husband Mark had been running the homestead for the past five years. As she finished speaking she glanced out of the window and saw her husband riding towards the house. Minutes later he dismounted and looked curiously at the three horses standing at the hitching-rail. Then he went into the house.

He stopped abruptly as his wife ran towards him and he saw the angry bruise on her face. He looked hard at Jack.

Quickly, his wife explained to him what had happened. His face flushed with anger as she told him of the vicious attack on herself. When she had finished he turned to Jack.

'We're mighty obliged to you, stranger,' he said.

'Glad I happened by when I did,' said Jack. 'My name's Tracy, Jack Tracy. About those two men in the barn. Maybe we can arrange for their wounds to be tended to and for the law to pick them up.'

'There's a doctor in Barlow, five miles west of here,' said Farren. 'If you don't mind staying here with Jane I'll ride there now and get him to come out here. At the same time I'll get a message sent to the law to come and pick up the two prisoners as soon as they can.'

'I'll be glad to hang on here till you get back,' said Jack.

A little over two hours later Farren returned. He was accompanied by the doctor and also by a friend of his who had offered to help him guard the prisoners until the law arrived to pick them up.

The doctor extracted the bullets from the right arms of the two prisoners, then bandaged the wounds. The two men were then securely bound again and were left lying on the floor of the barn.

'I'm hoping those two get just what they deserve,' said the doctor just before leaving. 'A woman should be safe in her own home. One thing, those two ain't going to be anything like as handy with a right-hand sixgun as they used to be.'

Back in the house, after the doctor had gone, Jack told the Farrens and their friend of the events leading up to his visit to the homestead. He asked the Farrens if they had seen four riders anywhere in the vicinity, heading south, around the date on which his family had been murdered.

Farren was quick to reply.

'We're sorry about what's happened to your folks,' he said. 'I think maybe I've seen the men who did it. What you've just told us might explain something that's been puzzling me.

'On the far side of the Diamond J ranch, which is a little way south of here, I have a friend who's running a homestead. I visited him around the time your folks were killed and I rode back here over the Diamond J range. I rested for a while in a small grove of trees standing west of the ranch buildings, and on top of a low ridge running north to south. I could see the ranch buildings in the distance.'

Farren went on to tell Jack how he had seen four riders approaching from the north, one of them slumped forward in the saddle. They stopped halfway between the grove and the ranch buildings and one of the riders fired three rifle shots into the air, then waved his arms. Shortly after this a rider came out to them from the ranch buildings, and returned to the buildings a few minutes later. After a little while he came out to them again, this time driving a buckboard.

The rider who had appeared to have been wounded had been lifted on to the buckboard where he had been joined by the three other riders. The buckboard was driven to the ranch buildings, while the man who had brought it out mounted one of the horses and led the other three off to the south. As the buckboard moved slowly back to the ranch house the two men sitting on the back used two long-handled brooms in an effort to remove the tracks made by the buckboard.

'At the time,' said Farren, 'I just couldn't figure out what was going on, but it weren't none of my business and I stayed out of sight.'

'It looks like they didn't know you were watching them from the grove,' said Jack.

'That's right,' said Farren. 'I rode into the trees from the west side of the ridge.'

'It all fits,' said Jack. 'Those four riders must be the ones who killed my folks. And it's clear that the man who rode off with the four horses was laying a false trail. What d'you know about the owner of the Diamond J?'

'Not much,' the homesteader replied. 'He's a man called Wayne Daley. Don't know where he came from. He set up the ranch about two years ago. It ain't a big spread. What I do know is that casual visitors ain't welcome there.

Anybody coming close to the ranch house is sure to be met by a couple of armed hands, and is turned away if he has no business there.'

'I'm going to the Diamond J,' said Jack. 'I'm hoping the four men I'm after are still there. I don't want to bring the law in until I'm certain of that. I'll be obliged if you don't say anything to anybody about those four men arriving at the Diamond J.'

'You can count on that,' said Farren, and the other two nodded assent.

Jack accepted the Farrens' invitation to spend the night there. In the morning he took his leave of them and headed for the Diamond J. He was halfway there when he heard a shout from behind and the sound of a rider coming up fast. He stopped, turned his mount, and waited.

As the horse came up to him and stopped, Jack saw that the rider was a young woman. Slim, raven-haired and good-looking, she was dressed in riding-clothes of good quality. She carried a Colt .45 on her right hip and a Winchester rifle in a saddle holster.

'Mr Tracy?' she asked.

'That's me,' Jack replied, curious about the identity of the young woman.

'I'm Ruth Mailer,' she said. 'The Farrens told me where I might find you. I called in at their homestead not long after you'd left, to find out if they'd seen you.

'I heard in Pueblo about your folks being murdered by the Laredo gang, and when I rode down to your ranch, your foreman told me you'd taken off after them. That's why I'm here.'

'I'm a mite curious as to why you want to see me so bad,' said Jack.

'Because we're both facing exactly the same problem,' she said, 'and that is to find the Laredo gang and make them pay for the murders of innocent people.'

'You've got a personal interest in this?' asked Jack.

'I have,' she replied. 'My father ran a small ranch in Wyoming. Just over a year ago he was on a stagecoach not far from Cheyenne. It was held up by the Laredo gang, and when my father protested about them stealing a woman passenger's wedding ring, the leader of the gang shot him dead. My mother never got over the shock and she died six weeks ago. That's when I decided to go after the gang. I sold the ranch and went to visit an aunt in Pueblo. The day after I got there I heard about the gang visiting the Box T, and your foreman told me you were going after the gang. I figured that maybe we could team up and do the job together, so's we don't get in one another's way.'

Jack looked into the face of the slender woman in front of him. On it was a look of grim determination to complete the task she had set herself. He admired her grit.

'I can see you're set on going after the gang,' said Jack, 'and you must know the danger you're going to be in. I see you're carrying a sixgun. D'you know how to use it?'

'Try me,' she said.

They dismounted. Jack picked up a stone about the size of his fist and threw it along the ground. It came to rest fourteen yards away.

'See if you can hit that,' he said.

Quickly and smoothly she drew the gun from its holster, pulling back the hammer as she did so, and fired the gun when it was just above hip level. The stone jerked backwards a few feet and came to rest. She fired three further shots in succession and three times the stone moved further away.

'You've had a good teacher,' said Jack.

'It was an uncle of mine who came to see us now and then,' said Ruth. 'Before he retired he was a deputy marshal. He gave me lessons in handling a sixgun and he reckoned I was a natural. And I'm pretty fair with the Winchester too.'

'All right,' said Jack, 'so long as you understand what we're up against, we'll work together. And I'm mighty glad of your help.'

He went on to tell Ruth of the four men, one injured, arriving at the Diamond J ranch, and of his conviction that they were the members of the Laredo gang. He described his plan to visit the ranch and establish whether the gang was there.

'If they are there,' said Jack, 'I want to get word to the law to come and pick them up. And that's where you can help. In sight of the Diamond J ranch house, and west of it, there's a small grove of trees on top of a low ridge. You can hide there while I go to the ranch house. You can get into the grove without being seen.'

He handed her a pair of field glasses.

'You keep watch from the grove during daylight,' he said, 'and I'll signal you if I find out that the gang is there. Then you can get the law down here and I'll help from the inside when they turn up. As for the signal I send you, that's something we have to decide on.'

'How about you taking your hat off and slapping it against your leg three times,' suggested Ruth, 'like you were knocking the dust out of it?'

'A good idea,' said Jack. 'That's what I'll do.'

'I'd no idea when I set out after you that I'd get close to the gang so quickly,' said Ruth. 'It's real good news you've given me.'

'I was lucky,' said Jack.

After a final brief discussion about their plan of action, Jack and Ruth parted. Jack's destination was the Diamond J. Ruth set off on a route which would bring her into the grove from the west.

When Jack came in sight of the ranch buildings he headed straight for them. He was still some distance away when two riders came in view, heading towards him. As they drew closer he could see that each of them was carrying a holstered sixgun. They stopped in front of Jack, blocking his way. He came to a halt.

The two men facing him were Harvey and Lander, two tough-looking characters bearing little resemblance to the ordinary ranch hand.

'What's your business here?' asked Harvey curtly.

'I'd like a few words with Mr Daley,' Jack replied.

'What about?' asked Harvey. 'Tell me, and I'll find out if he wants to see you.'

'All right,' said Jack, 'if that's the way he wants it. Tell him I'd like a chat with him about four riders, one of them injured, who stopped near here not that long ago, and were picked up by a Diamond J buckboard.'

Startled, the two men facing Jack glanced at each other. Then Harvey spoke.

'Stay here,' he said, 'while I check with Mr Daley. Move from this spot and you'll get a rifle bullet in you.'

Twenty minutes later the two men reappeared and rode out to Jack again.

'Ride in front of us,' said Harvey, 'up to the door of the ranch house.'

As they neared the house it struck

Jack how much larger it was than the average house on a ranch of this size.

On reaching the house he dismounted and was ushered into a large living-room in which a man was standing facing him. The man was well-dressed, of medium height, and a little overweight. He had a hard face, with a florid complexion. He told the two hands to wait outside in case they were needed. Then he studied Jack for a few moments, before speaking.

'I'm Daley,' he said. 'What's this cock-and-bull story you've been telling my men?'

'There ain't nothing cock-and-bull about it,' Jack replied. 'It's all true. It's exactly what I saw when I was resting in the shade of that grove of trees west of here. Four riders came along and were taken up to the ranch buildings on a buckboard.

'I didn't think much of it at the time and I rode on. Then, a couple of days later, I heard that the Laredo gang, with one man injured, had been chased over the Wyoming border into Colorado, and had disappeared, leaving four stolen horses a little way south of here. So I'm pretty sure it was the Laredo gang that I saw on that buckboard.

'The reason I'm here today is because I'd like to meet the leader of the gang to see if I can join up with them. I've heard about the big hauls they've made, and I'm tired of working on my own, with mighty little to show for it.'

Daley, who had been studying Jack and listening intently to what he was saying, spoke.

'Did it occur to you,' he asked, 'that if the Laredo gang did happen to be here and they got to know that you'd seen them arriving, then you'd be as good as dead?'

'I don't see it that way,' said Jack. 'I don't wish the gang no harm. If I did, I'd have gone straight to the law and claimed the reward. The law and me ain't exactly friends. All I want is the chance to join up with the gang. I like the way they work.'

'It's a dangerous game you're playing,' said Daley. 'Stay here. I'll take your sixgun. Don't move out of this room. If you do, you'll be cut down.'

Jack handed his gun over and Daley left the room. When he returned fifteen minutes later, he was accompanied by four men, one of them carrying his right arm in a sling. They all sat down and Daley motioned to Jack to do the same.

Instinctively, Jack knew that he was looking at the four members of the infamous Laredo gang. He steeled himself to show no emotion as he studied them one by one. Unknown to him, their names were Craig, their leader, Slater, Carney and Chandler.

Craig was a slim man, a little over average height, with a long, cruel face, black eyes, and a knife-scar running down his left cheek. Right away Jack guessed that he was the leader.

Slater, scowling as his eyes met Jack's, was a stocky man of medium height, balding, with bushy eyebrows. Carney, his arm in a sling, and Chandler, were complete opposites in appearance. Carney, taller than Craig, was heavily built, with massive shoulders. Chandler, only an inch or two over five feet, was slim and wiry, with a slight cast in one eye. All four men, Jack guessed, were in their late thirties.

Craig spoke abruptly. 'What's your name?' he asked.

'Fisher,' replied Jack, 'Bert Fisher.'

'Well, Fisher,' said Craig, 'the only reason you're still alive is that I'm curious to hear from your own lips just why you came here.'

'Like I said,' Jack replied. 'I ain't been doing too good on my own in Kansas. I figured I'd be better off in a gang where somebody else did the thinking for me.'

Craig studied Jack for a few moments before he replied.

'I'm Craig,' he said. 'I'm the leader of the gang.'

He introduced the three men who

had come in with him. Then he continued.

'It so happens,' he said, 'that I'm planning a big job in the Texas Panhandle that I need some more men for. I've sent for two good men I know in West Kansas. I can use you as well.'

It was now dark outside and Craig glanced at the clock on the wall.

'There's a room here in the house that you can use,' he said, 'and you can take supper in the cookshack in about an hour. Listen for the call. Tomorrow we'll see how good you are with a sixgun and a rifle, and you can tell us all about the jobs you've pulled off in Kansas.'

Daley took Jack to his room.

'I'll have your horse seen to,' he said, 'and I'd advise you not to leave the house on your own while it's dark. I have armed guards out there who're liable to shoot at anything that moves in the dark.'

Daley returned to Craig and the others.

'Maybe Fisher's lying, maybe he's not,' said Craig. 'For the time being, Daley, have a close watch kept on him and make sure he's stopped if he tries to leave.'

Jack stayed in his room till he heard the call for supper. He went to the cookshack through a covered passage from the house. Slater, Carney and Chandler were seated at the table, together with ten other men who looked curiously at Jack. He took no part in the conversation around the table, and returned to his room when the meal was over. He had decided that he would signal Ruth after breakfast the following morning.

3

When Jack went for breakfast at the time given him by Daley, he found the cookshack deserted, except for the cook, who told him he was the last one to be served. When he had finished the meal he went back to his room to collect his hat.

When he rode in on the previous day he had noticed the look-out stationed on a platform on the roof of the house, and he knew that when he left it his movements would be closely watched. Looking from the grove through field glasses, he and Ruth had located a place near the house from which Jack could send the signal. Standing there, wearing a light-coloured vest, he would be clearly visible to Ruth.

He decided to signal Ruth as soon as possible. He opened the door of his room and stopped short as he was confronted by Craig and Daley. Each of them was holding a sixgun in his hand.

'Let's go outside, Fisher,' said Craig. 'Something mighty interesting has just happened and we figured you'd like to know about it. You lead the way. And don't forget about these two guns on your back.'

Jack walked out of the door of the house, with the two men close behind him, then he stopped abruptly. In front of him, her hands bound, stood Ruth. Two ranch hands were holding her arms. As she looked at Jack, he could see the anger and despair in her eyes. Slater and Chandler came out of the house and Craig told them to hold their guns on Jack. Then he and Daley walked round to face the prisoner.

'I have a feeling, Fisher,' said Craig, 'that you know the woman over there. The look-out spotted a reflection of sunlight from her field glasses in that grove over there, and I sent some men out to circle round to the back of the grove and pick her up.

'You turn up yesterday, then we find the woman spying on us today. It's too much of a coincidence. You two must be working together. I want to know who you are and why you're here. It looks like you ain't got nothing to do with the law. I'm sure we can find some way of getting the truth out of you.'

Jack's and Ruth's belongings were all examined but they gave no clues to their identities or the reason for their presence.

Looking to the west Craig saw a rider approaching.

'Looks like Ward,' he said. 'We'll wait till he gets here.'

When the rider reached him Craig took him aside and they had a brief conversation. Then Craig returned to Daley.

'There's no time to deal with these two now,' he said. 'Ward's brought news about the operation. Put them in that storage shed behind the bunkhouse. Tie them up and put a guard outside.'

Craig went into the house with the

other three members of the gang. Ward and Daley accompanied them. Jack and Ruth were taken to the small storage shed, where their hands and feet were bound, and they were left sitting on the floor of the shed, with their backs to the wall. The door was bolted on the outside and an armed guard was posted close to the shed.

Jack turned his head to look at the woman sitting beside him.

'You all right, Ruth?' he asked. 'They didn't harm you?'

'No,' Ruth replied. 'When I saw those riders leave the ranch buildings I had no idea they were going to circle round and come up behind me. I was so busy watching out for your signal that they were right on me before I realized they were there.'

'You've probably guessed,' said Jack, 'that the Laredo gang is here. The man who was talking to me a minute or two ago is Craig, the leader. When I came out of the house I was getting ready to signal you. It was just a stroke of luck for them, picking up the reflection from the glasses.'

'What happens now?' asked Ruth.

'I've got to say,' Jack replied, 'that I reckon Craig has it in mind to kill us both. Just when and where I don't know. But while we're alive, there's still a slim chance we can save ourselves.'

★　★　★

Inside the house Craig and his men were receiving a report from Ward, who had been sent to look over a bank in the Texas Panhandle which the gang was planning to rob when Carney's wound had healed. When Ward had finished his report they discussed the matter of Jack's arrival and the discovery of Ruth.

'I think I know who they are,' said Ward. 'I called in at a small town yesterday, just after a stage had passed through, and the folks there were talking about something the driver had told them. He'd said that a man called

Tracy and a woman called Mailer were both trying to locate the Laredo gang, on account of the gang murdering Craig's parents and brother, and the woman's father. It looks to me like they teamed up, and they're the ones locked up in the shed.'

'So that's it,' said Craig. 'I think I know where they're both from. It could be that other people suspect that the gang might be here. We'll have to move out now. We'll go to the hideout in the Texas Panhandle and stay there till the job's done.'

Craig confirmed with Carney that he was fit to ride, then he turned to Daley, who managed the ranch for him. As owner, Craig made a sizable profit from the cattle-raising operation, as well as using the ranch as a headquarters and hideout for the gang.

'Ward and Arnold can take care of the two prisoners,' he told Daley, knowing that the two men had no qualms about killing, and would be satisfied with the bonus he was prepared to give them.

'I want them killed well away from here,' he went on, 'and I want it to look like an accident. I'm leaving it to you to arrange all the details. Ward and Arnold had better leave with them just after dark.'

The gang rode out just under an hour later. Before leaving, Craig looked in on the prisoners. Grinning, he looked down on them.

'Mr Tracy and Miss Mailer, I believe,' he said. 'Just called in to let you know that we're leaving now. You'll be taking a ride yourselves later today, and the ride you take will be your last. You were fools to think you could take on the Laredo gang.'

When Craig had left, the prisoners were silent for a while. Then Ruth spoke. Her face was strained, but her voice was steady.

'Looks like our future ain't too bright, Jack,' she said.

'It looks that way,' said Jack, 'but until we're dead there's always a chance that we'll get free. No need to give up just yet.'

After the gang had left, Daley called Ward and Arnold into the house to discuss the disposal of the two prisoners. He described in detail exactly where and how he wanted them killed.

Shortly after sunset the prisoners' feet were untied and they were led to their saddled horses which were standing outside the house. The items previously taken from their pockets and saddlebags were replaced. They were ordered to mount and their hands were tied behind them. Ward and Arnold mounted their horses and led the two prisoners off to the south-east.

They rode on through the night and just as dawn was breaking they reached a deep, narrow gorge which cut across their path. Jack judged that by now they were well into the Texas Panhandle. Ward dismounted and looked down into the gorge. Below him he could see water rushing through gaps between the large boulders littering the bed of the gorge. From the position where Ward was standing the ground sloped steeply down for a short distance before meeting the top of the sheer wall of the gorge.

Ward walked over to Jack, pulled him down from his horse, and ordered him to lie face down on the ground.

'Don't try anything,' he said. 'If you do, your partner gets a bullet through the head.'

He wound a length of rope around Jack's legs and upper body, encircling the arms. All the turns were pulled tight, and one end of the rope was left free. Then Ward removed the rope holding Jack's hands together.

Ruth was now dealt with in exactly the same way as Jack. Then the two prisoners were dragged near to the point from which Ward had looked down into the gorge. Arnold and Ward walked out of earshot of the prisoners and started a conversation. Jack took the opportunity of talking in a whisper with Ruth.

'I'm sure they're going to drop us in the gorge, Ruth,' he said. 'I guess they'll roll us down over the edge while they hang on to the end of the rope. But before they do that I think they'll knock us senseless. That's the only way they can be sure we'll die. Our only chance is to roll down into the gorge before they come back here. Can you do that, Ruth?'

'I can do it,' Ruth replied, her voice shaking. 'I can do it, but I'm scared to death. When do we go?'

'Right now,' said Jack. 'Let's go down together. Take a deep breath just before you hit the water. And you're not the only one who's scared.'

Just as Ward and Arnold finished their conversation and started walking back towards their prisoners, Jack and Ruth started rolling down the slope. Before the two men above could reach the spot where the prisoners had been lying they had disappeared from view and were dropping vertically towards the bottom of the gorge. During their descent the turns of rope around their bodies had loosened, and as Jack hit the water and sank below the surface he was frantically ridding himself of the coils around his body. When he had done this he rose to the surface and looked around for Ruth.

A moment later he saw her just upstream of him in the fast-flowing water. Her arms were free, but her legs were still held by the rope. She was coughing the water out of her lungs and beating the surface with her arms. Jack swam up to her and supported her head clear of the water as they were swept downstream close to the vertical wall of the gorge. They were out of sight of the two men above.

'So much for knocking them both out before we dropped them into the gorge,' said Arnold.

'Can't see that it matters,' said Ward. 'It's a long drop and you can see all them boulders down there. They don't stand a chance. There's no need to say anything to Daley about what happened.'

What the two men could not see from where they were standing was that an unobstructed channel, a few feet wide, stretched out from the sheer wall of the gorge. It was into this channel that the two prisoners had fallen.

Ward and Arnold made a small fire and took a meal. They left a coffee-pot and two mugs standing near the fire, and on the ground nearby they left a canvas bag containing some food. They removed all traces of their own presence there, and rode off towards the Diamond J, leaving behind the two horses which had been ridden by Jack and Ruth.

★   ★   ★

Down in the gorge Jack and Ruth were carried along by the fast-flowing water. The channel they were in had narrowed and from time to time they were dashed against half-submerged boulders, suffering small cuts and bruises in the process. But Jack kept a tight hold on

Ruth and unwound the rope from her legs.

Soon the river widened and the sheer walls of the gorge gave way to banks which rose for only a short distance above the surface of the water. Jack swam towards a bank and close to it his feet touched the river bed. He lifted Ruth on to the top of the bank, then climbed out himself. For a while they both lay there, exhausted. Then Ruth spoke.

'That was a close one,' she said. 'For a while there I thought I was a goner.'

'We were lucky, falling into that deep channel,' said Jack. 'I doubt if Ward and his partner knew it was there. They'll figure us for dead. How're you feeling, Ruth?'

'Pretty battered,' she replied. 'But nothing's broken.'

'Same here,' said Jack, as he started to rise to his feet. Then he stiffened as he looked along the river bank downstream and caught sight of two approaching riders.

'We've got company,' he said. Ruth rose to stand by his side. The two riders came up to them and halted. They were both bearded and unkempt, giving the impression that they had been living rough and had spent many hours in the saddle. In fact, both men were outlaws, with no regard for human life. Morton, the elder of the two, was a big man with sandy hair. His companion, Leary, was short and slender, but he looked just as hard and ruthless as his partner. The two men had been riding through Kansas recently, and had called briefly at a small settlement. A deputy sheriff, who just happened to be there at the time had recognized them. He raised a posse and chased them until they crossed the border into the Indian territory.

Now, as they approached the man and woman standing on the river bank, they looked at them with some curiosity. They noted that their clothing was wet and that they did not appear to be armed and were apparently on foot.

Both the riders dismounted.

'You folks look like you're in real trouble,' said Morton. 'What happened to you?'

'We were walking on the bank well upstream,' said Jack, 'when the ground gave way and we fell into the water. We've only just managed to get out. We were due to meet up with five of my ranch hands there, and any time now they'll be along here looking for us.'

The two outlaws both looked upstream for any approaching riders.

'There's nobody in sight,' said Morton. 'I think you're lying. We figure there's a posse out looking for us and we don't want them to find out that we've been seen in this area.'

Quickly, Morton drew one of the two sixguns he was carrying, and Leary drew the single gun that he was wearing.

'This means,' Morton continued, 'that you two will have to die.'

He spoke to Leary, so quietly that Jack and Ruth could not hear his words.

'Keep the man well covered,' he said, 'but don't fire unless you really have to. We don't want to draw anybody here just now. It's a long time since we had female company, and I've a mind to get better acquainted with the lady. Later on, just before we leave, we'll shoot them both dead and drop them in the river.'

Leaving Leary to cover Jack, Morton holstered his sixgun and walked up to Ruth, grabbed her firmly by the arms, and dragged her several paces away from Jack. Then he tried to force her to the ground. Ruth resisted vigorously and kicked him hard on the shin. Cursing, he was about to strike her with his fist when, as she looked upstream over his shoulder, he heard her shout.

'Jack!' she yelled. 'The hands are coming.'

Morton twisted round, momentarily releasing his grip on Ruth. She pulled both his sixguns out of the holsters and stepped back. She threw one gun towards Jack, and with the other she shot Morton in the chest as he advanced on her. The outlaw collapsed on the ground.

Leary had also been distracted by Ruth's call, and Jack had time to catch the sixgun by the handle, dodge Leary's bullet, and shoot him through the heart.

Jack checked that both men were dead. Then he walked over to Ruth, who was staring down at the two bodies on the ground. She was trembling, unnerved by the events of the last few minutes. He put his arms around her while she recovered. Then he spoke.

'That was quick thinking, Ruth,' he said. 'I reckon you saved both our lives. Don't feel too bad about killing a man. There's no doubt in my mind that it was either them or us. I wonder who these two are.'

He searched the two men for some indication of their identities. All he could find was a telegraph message addressed to: MOLE. BAR 10 RANCH GRANTON KANSAS. It read: NEED TWO

MEN FOR BIG OPERATION AMARILLO TEXAS PANHANDLE SOON AS POSSIBLE. WILL MEET AT CABIN. CRAIG

Jack read the message twice, then walked over to Ruth and showed it to her.

'I have a notion, Ruth,' he said, when she had finished reading the message, 'that the Craig who sent this is the leader of the Laredo gang. He told me he had sent for two friends of his in Kansas to help him out on a job in the Texas Panhandle. And now we know that the job they're planning will be done in Amarillo.'

He looked at the two bodies on the ground.

'There's plenty of stones lying around,' he said. 'I'll drag those two back a piece from the river, and we'll cover them over. We'll keep their guns and ammunition, as well as their money.'

'And what do we do after that?' asked Ruth.

'I reckon we'll find our horses near

the place where we fell into the gorge,'
Jack replied. 'We'll ride there on these
men's horses, then head straight for
Amarillo to see if we can locate the
Laredo gang. Is that all right with you,
Ruth?'

'Just what I was thinking myself,' she
said.

It was a warm day, and they dried
their clothing as best they could. Then,
after covering the two bodies, they rode
back to the place where they had
dropped into the gorge. They found
their horses standing nearby. After
eating some of the food left behind by
the two Diamond J hands, they headed
south for Amarillo, leading the mounts
of the two dead outlaws.

They camped out overnight, and the
following morning, after an hour's
ride, they reached the small town of
Chilver. They went into the store for
provisions. Jack told the storekeeper
about their encounter with the two
outlaws, and asked him to report it to
the next law officer who turned up. He

said that he and Ruth were on their way to see the US marshal in Amarillo. After leaving the outlaws' horses at the livery stable, they took a meal, then left town.

4

When Craig and the other members of his gang left the Diamond J, they headed for a ravine north of Amarillo, and not far off the main trail leading to Amarillo from the north. In the ravine was an abandoned log cabin which the gang had used as a hideout on several occasions in the past. There was water running down the ravine. Upstream from the cabin was a waterfall, and the sides of the ravine were steeply sloped, so that riders could only approach the cabin from below.

When Craig and the others arrived at the cabin they found it empty, with no indication that anyone had stayed there recently. They settled down to await the arrival of Morton and Leary, whom they expected to arrive sometime during the next few days. A look-out was posted on top of the sloping side of the ravine to watch out for approaching riders.

Craig had reliable information from a Wells Fargo employee in his pay, that a Wells Fargo express wagon carrying a gold shipment worth $200,000 would be in the area in about nine days' time. It was scheduled to drive down from the north, call briefly at Amarillo, then continue on to the Gulf of Mexico, where the gold would be transferred to a ship.

The wagon would carry a driver and armed Wells Fargo guards. Craig had already selected the spot where the robbery would take place. It was fourteen miles north of Amarillo, where the trail passed between two tall rocky outcrops.

Two days after the arrival of the gang at the cabin, Slater was at the look-out point. Just after midday he saw two distant riders moving south along the trail to Amarillo. As they drew closer he got the impression that they were a man and a woman. He picked up a pair of field glasses and trained them on the two riders, and confirmed this.

As they passed the point nearest to him he stiffened and examined them closely through the glasses. When he was sure of what he was looking at, he hurried down into the ravine and along to the cabin where Craig was seated with Chandler and Carney.

'You ain't going to believe this,' he said, as they looked at him in surprise. 'There's a couple of riders heading south along the trail out there. One's Tracy and the other is the woman Mailer.'

'You sure?' asked Craig, as he and the others rose to their feet.

'Plumb sure,' Slater replied. 'I recognized them *and* their horses.'

'Damn Daley!' said Craig. 'How in hell do those two come to be free?'

Quickly, he considered the situation, before speaking to the others.

'Were they riding fast?' he asked Slater.

'No,' replied Slater, 'just slow and steady.'

'Right,' said Craig. 'We'll all ride as fast as we can to the spot where we're going to rob the express wagon. If we ride behind that ridge over there, and head south, we'll be out of sight of Tracy. We've got to finish them off. They know too much about us, including the fact that we're planning a job in the Texas Panhandle. It could be they're going to tell the lawmen in Amarillo everything they know about us. Let's go.'

Riding as fast as they were able without overtaxing their mounts, Craig and the others reached the two outcrops. Looking through field glasses, Craig could see no sign of the two riders they intended to ambush.

'They could be a while yet,' he said. 'Maybe they'll be taking a meal and a rest somewhere along the way.'

★   ★   ★

The day before Jack and Ruth were spotted by Slater, they had been riding south towards Amarillo. They stopped and rested for a while just off the trail, at a point about six miles north of the Laredo gang's hideout. They discussed what they would do when they reached Amarillo.

'The thing to do first,' said Jack, 'is call on the US marshal there. I was assigned to him for four days a while back when he was passing through the Indian Territory. His name's Dixon. He's highly respected as a law officer. We'll tell him all we know about the gang.'

They mounted and had ridden on a few hundred yards when Jack caught sight of two animals off to the left, well back from the trail and standing near the foot of a ridge. The animals were not horses or cows, but looked more like mules or *burros*. He drew Ruth's attention to them.

'Don't see anybody moving anywhere near them,' he said. 'Maybe somebody's in trouble. Let's take a look.'

They left the trail and rode towards

the two animals. As they drew closer they could see that they were a mule and a *burro*. The latter was obviously being used as a prospector's pack-animal.

'Likely there's a prospector around here somewhere,' said Jack, 'but where?'

Ruth pointed to the foot of the ridge, a short distance away.

'Looks like an opening at the bottom of the ridge,' she said. 'Maybe he's in there.'

'Let's take a look,' said Jack.

They rode up to the ridge and dismounted outside the entrance to a mine-shaft which gave every indication of having been abandoned long ago. Looking at the ground Jack saw fresh footprints leading into the shaft. He and Ruth followed the footprints into the shaft, which took a slightly downward direction. Only a few yards from the entrance their way was barred by what looked like a recent collapse of the roof of the shaft.

'There's a man under that pile, or on

the other side of it,' said Jack. 'Stand well back while I go and get the shovel from the *burro*.'

When Jack returned he started removing rubble from the top of the pile. Ruth helped him. After a time they came upon a pair of heavy timber support beams. As they paused for a moment they heard a faint groan coming from under the beams. Redoubling their efforts, they removed the beams which had firmly pinned down the man who was lying beneath them.

Lying on his back, half-dazed, prospector Hank Keeler looked up at his rescuers. He was a stocky man, nudging sixty, his face deep brown from long exposure to sun and wind. An angry bruise showed on his forehead. 'You all right?' asked Jack.

Keeler who, except for a short spell as an Army scout in the Indian Wars, had been prospecting all his adult life, shook his head to clear it and looked up at Ruth and Jack.

'I was a danged fool,' he said, 'to walk

along the shaft. That roof was just waiting to come down. When it did, something hit me hard on the head.'

Gingerly, he moved his arms and legs.

'Otherwise I seem to be OK,' he went on. 'It sure was lucky for me you happened along. I couldn't free myself and I was running out of air to breathe.'

Jack helped Keeler to his feet and they all walked out into the open, where Ruth cleaned and bandaged the wound on the prospector's head.

When she had finished, Jack spoke to Keeler.

'It'll be dark soon,' he said. 'We'll stay with you overnight to make sure you're all right. That was a nasty bang you got on the head.'

'I'd be obliged,' said Keeler. 'I'll be glad of the company.'

The following morning, after breakfast, they spent some time talking to Keeler, who seemed to be recovering from his ordeal in the shaft. Jack told him that they were going to Amarillo to try and locate the Laredo gang. He explained why and said they were pretty sure that the gang was in the area.

'I aim to be in Amarillo myself in a week or so,' said Keeler, 'after I've taken a look at one or two places south of here.'

Jack and Ruth took their leave of Keeler, and some time later they were observed by Slater, on look-out at the gang's hideout. They rode on for a few miles, before calling at the small town of Blaney where they bought some provisions. Then they rode on towards Amarillo.

Eventually they came in sight of two tall rocky outcrops between which the trail passed. As they rode between them they suddenly stopped short as four men, all holding guns, ran out in front of them. The two riders recognized Craig and his men. They realized that any resistance would be suicidal. Slater walked up and took the prisoners' weapons. Then he went for the gang's horses. Craig looked at the two captives. His face was hard.

'I never figured to see you two alive again,' he said, 'but we sure ain't going to make any mistake this time.'

He spoke to Carney and Chandler who were holding their guns on the captives.

'We badly need to know,' he said, 'how these two got free, what they're doing here, and what information they've passed on to the law about us. We'll cram them in that little shed near the cabin and leave them there without food and water until Morton and Leary get here. You know what Morton's like. If anybody can get the information out of them, it's him.'

Slater returned with the horses. The prisoners' hands were tied, and the six riders left for the hideout.

★ ★ ★

At about the same time that Jack and Ruth were being ambushed by the Laredo gang, Hank Keeler rode his mule into the ravine where the Laredo gang was hiding out. He had visited the ravine once before, several years ago, and had stayed in the cabin for a short spell while he looked around the area. But when he went into the cabin this time, it was clear, from the contents, that it was in use, seemingly by four people who might return at any time.

Keeler was a cautious man. He knew there was a possibility that the occupants of the cabin were criminals who, if they found him there, would not take kindly to his presence. He rode back down the ravine until he was able to ride up the sloping side of the ravine to the top. He rode back along the top until he reached a small grove of trees from the cover of which he could look down on the cabin. He dismounted and led the mule and the *burro* into the grove.

An inquisitive man by nature, he decided to stay under cover and watch the occupants of the cabin for a while when they returned. If he did not like the look of them he would leave.

There was still an hour to go before nightfall when Keeler saw six riders approaching the cabin. When they reached it, four of them dismounted. Keeler looked hard at the other two. They looked familiar. A glance at their horses confirmed his suspicion that they were the two who had come to his rescue in the mine-shaft the previous day.

As Keeler watched, Jack and Ruth were roughly pulled out of their saddles and their arms were tightly bound to their sides. Then Carney and Slater took turns at punching Jack savagely around the head and body until he collapsed on the ground. They gave him a few final kicks, then he was pulled to his feet and he and Ruth were taken to the small shed near the cabin. A few pieces of timber were taken out, then the prisoners were pushed in and the door was bolted on the outside.

As Keeler watched he began to

suspect that by some mischance Jack and Ruth had been captured by the very gang they had been searching for. He could see that the shed was barely large enough to accommodate the two prisoners, both standing erect. As he continued to watch he saw six horses led to a picket line and the four men walk into the cabin, leaving the door open behind them.

Just before darkness fell one man left the cabin and took up a position outside the shed. Obviously a guard, thought Keeler.

Four hours later, the prospector saw the door of the lighted cabin open as a man went inside. Almost immediately another man left the cabin, closing the door behind him. A few minutes later the light in the cabin went out. A half-moon was showing and patches of cloud were moving slowly across the sky.

Half an hour later, Keeler left the grove on foot, retracing the route he had followed earlier from the cabin to the grove. He was carrying a double-barrelled shotgun. Moving silently up the ravine, and taking advantage of a cloud which was passing over the moon, he reached a position behind the shed containing the prisoners. On the other side Chandler was standing.

Keeler laid his shotgun on the ground, then threw a stone which landed halfway between the shed and the cabin.

Chandler stiffened, listened for a moment, then took a couple of steps towards the cabin. Keeler drew a long double-edged knife from his belt, silently moved round the shed, and came up behind Chandler. He drove his knife hard and deep into the outlaw's back. Chandler gave a strangled shout before he collapsed on the ground and lay there motionless. Keeler retrieved his knife, then opened the door of the shed and led Ruth and Jack round to the back, where he untied the ropes which had been used to secure them.

Keeler told Jack and Ruth that the

man who had been guarding the shed was dead. He also told them that he had been watching from the grove when the outlaws arrived at the ravine with their prisoners.

'That man I knifed probably has a sixgun on him,' he said. 'Wait here while I get it. I brought a shotgun with me. It's on the ground there.'

He moved round the shed, walked up to Chandler, and took a sixgun from its holster. He turned and started walking back towards Jack and Ruth.

Inside the cabin Craig, a light sleeper, had been woken by the strangled shout from Chandler. He lay for a while wondering what it was that had disturbed him. Remembering the prisoners in the shed, he rose from his bunk, picked up his sixgun, and ran over to the only window, which was adjacent to the cabin door. He opened the shutters and looked towards the shed.

In the moonlight he saw a body lying on the ground near the shed, and a man walking away from the body. He fired two shots at the man, who fell down by the side of the shed, and was quickly dragged behind it by Jack. The sixgun, which had fallen from Keeler's hand was then retrieved by Jack, who fired two shots through the cabin window, narrowly missing Craig. Then Jack, still suffering from the effects of the savage beating he had received, knelt down by Keeler and felt his pulse.

'He's dead, Ruth,' he said. 'He sure had plenty of grit, coming into the ravine to save us like that. Damn those men in the cabin.'

He picked up the prospector's shotgun and checked that it was fully loaded. Then he went through the prospector's pockets and found six more cartridges. He handed the shotgun and cartridges to Ruth.

'I'm going to the horses, Ruth,' he said. 'We'll ride out of the ravine and take their horses with us. You stay here while I get the horses ready to move. While I'm gone, fire a shotgun blast towards the cabin door and window every few minutes, but save two cartridges. I'll call for you to come to me as soon as I'm ready.'

When Ruth heard Jack's call she fired a last shot towards the cabin before joining him near the picket line. She handed him the shotgun, loaded with the last two cartridges. Then they both mounted and, with Jack leading the four outlaws' horses, they rode fast down the ravine. As they approached the cabin Jack fired the shotgun towards it twice and Ruth sent two bullets from the sixgun into the door.

Before the men in the cabin realized what had happened, Jack and Ruth had passed the cabin, and had ridden out of the ravine, leaving them without horses. After picking up Keeler's mule and *burro* from the grove, Jack and Ruth headed for Blaney.

They arrived there in the early hours of the morning. Jack hammered on the door of the hotel, which was locked. After a while it was opened by Lorimer, the owner, who invited them inside. Jack told him about their recent escape from the Laredo gang, taking the gang's horses with them.

'I need to send a telegraph message to the US marshal in Amarillo,' he said. 'Those three men we left in the ravine are dangerous killers. Marshal Dixon will jump at the chance of capturing them. I figure that they'd leave the ravine soon after we did. But they won't get far without mounts.'

'The telegraph office is just along the street,' said Lorimer, 'but the line ain't open till eight o'clock. I have a couple of rooms empty if you'd like them.'

Ruth looked at Jack's battered face.

'We'll take the rooms,' she said, 'but you can see my partner was beat up pretty bad. Can you let me have some warm water to clean up his face — and maybe a plaster or two.'

'Sure,' said Lorimer, 'and while you're doing that I'll whip up a meal for you. Then I'll put those animals you brought with you in a corral behind the livery stable.'

'We're obliged,' said Jack. 'The gang took some of our money, but I've got plenty in a hidden pocket in my saddle-bag. Keeler, the prospector who saved our lives, is lying dead in the ravine. Can you get the undertaker to pick him up and see him buried right? I'll foot the bill. He told us he has no kin alive.'

'I'll see to that,' said Lorimer.

Jack and Ruth were outside the telegraph office when it opened. They went inside, where Jack wrote down the message and showed it to Ruth. It was addressed to US Marshal Dixon in Amarillo. It read:

URGENT, ONE MEMBER LAREDO GANG KILLED IN RAVINE NORTH OF BLANEY EIGHT HOURS AGO. LEADER AND TWO OTHERS ON THE LOOSE. ARE ARMED BUT WITHOUT HORSES. NEED HELP. SEND LAWMEN TO MEET ME AT

HOTEL BLANEY. JACK TRACY EX-DEPUTY US MARSHAL INDIAN TERRITORY.

Jack handed the message to the telegraph operator who told him that an answer would probably be coming soon. He said he would bring it to the hotel as soon as he received it.

Jack and Ruth returned to the hotel for breakfast, during which Lorimer came in and handed to Jack the proceeds of the sale, to the livery stable owner, of the four horses which had belonged to the outlaws. After breakfast they went into the store and bought two rifles, a sixgun and some ammunition. As they left the store the telegraph operator ran up with the reply to their telegraph message. It read:

RANGER CAPTAIN HARPER SENDING THREE RANGERS TO RENDEZVOUS WITH YOU AT BLANEY. RANGER BRAND IN CHARGE. ARRIVING NOT LATER

THAN 3PM TODAY. DIXON US
MARSHAL.

The rangers arrived at 2.30. Brand
was accompanied by Rangers Laker
and Raglan. Over a quick meal in the
hotel Jack and Ruth told them of the
events leading to their escape during
the night from the Laredo gang. Ranger
Brand, a swarthy, capable-looking law
officer, asked Jack whether he was going
to ride with them after the three
outlaws.

'Sure,' Jack replied.

'Me too,' said Ruth.

Brand looked doubtful but Jack cut
in before he could speak.

'Miss Mailer can handle a sixgun and
a rifle just as well as most men I know,'
he said, 'and her father *was* murdered
by the gang.'

'We'll be glad to have both of you
along,' said Brand. 'We'd best be
leaving.'

'We're ready,' said Jack. 'We should
reach the ravine before nightfall. I asked

the hotel owner to arrange for Keeler's body to be picked up at the ravine, and a buckboard will be following us there. It can take Chandler's body back to town as well.'

When they reached the ravine they found the bodies of Keeler and Chandler still lying near the shed. There was no sign of the three outlaws.

Brand, whose tracking expertise was well known to his fellow rangers, studied the tracks on the ground inside the ravine, then walked out of it on to the flat ground beyond. Then he returned to the others, as darkness was falling. He told them that the three outlaws, on foot, had left the ravine and had struck off in a northerly direction.

'It's too dark to follow the tracks now,' he said. 'We'll have to wait till dawn.'

They set off at first light, Brand riding well ahead. The tracks continued north in an almost straight line. Just after noon, still following the clear tracks of the three outlaws, they approached a large solitary flat-topped rocky outcrop. When they had passed this, Brand, who was some way ahead, suddenly stopped, bent down to look more closely at the ground, then rode a short distance to the east before returning to the others.

'Looks like they picked up some horses here,' he said, 'and now they're riding to the east. Wait here.'

He dismounted and walked slowly towards the outcrop. As he drew near he started to circle it, then walked up to a deep narrow cleft in the side. He disappeared inside this and reappeared shortly after. He signalled the others to join him. When they reached him they sensed from the grim look on his face that something was wrong. They all dismounted.

'It's mighty bad news,' he said. 'There are three dead rangers in there, all shot in the back and the head. They're from Amarillo.'

Laker and Raglan went into the cleft.

'These dead men,' said Brand to Jack

and Ruth, 'were all partners of ours. They left Amarillo four days ago to try and locate a gang of cattle-rustlers operating north of here. It looks like they were ambushed by the Laredo gang so's they could steal their horses.'

He turned to Laker who, grim-faced and shaken, had just appeared from the cleft.

'Ride back to Blaney,' he said, 'and arrange to have these bodies picked up. And let Captain Harper know what's happened. The rest of us'll follow Craig and the others. But I figure they're heading for the Indian Territory and I guess they'll cross the border long before we catch up with them.'

And he was right. Following the tracks of the three horses, they reached the border with Indian Territory the following day.

'This is where we stop,' Brand told Jack and Ruth. 'We'll notify the US marshal in Fort Smith that Craig and the other two have crossed the border into his territory. We're sorry we have to give up the chase. Those three dead men back there were all good friends of ours. What are you two aiming to do now?'

'We'll follow them ourselves,' said Jack, and Ruth nodded agreement.

'We'll pass that information on to Fort Smith as well,' said Brand.

They parted company shortly after, and Jack and Ruth rode on into the Indian Territory.

5

Jack and Ruth followed the tracks of the outlaws' horses for several miles through the Indian Territory. Then they lost them.

'I ain't in the same class as Brand when it comes to tracking,' said Jack. 'We won't waste time trying to pick up the tracks again. We'll keep riding on in the same direction and maybe we'll meet up with somebody who's seen the three riders we're after.'

They rode on for a few hours after darkness had fallen, then started to look for a suitable campsite. They picked a spot, and Jack was just about to start a fire when he caught sight of a flicker of flame a little way off to the south-east. He drew Ruth's attention to it.

'It looks like a camp-fire,' he said. 'I suppose it's just possible that the men we're after are there. You stay here and

I'll sneak over to that fire on foot and take a look at whoever's there.'

'I'm going with you,' she said.

Resignedly, Jack shook his head and smiled. He knew it was useless to argue.

'You're an obstinate woman, Ruth,' he said. 'Let's go.'

They left the horses picketed and walked towards the distant light. They were both wearing a holstered sixgun. As they drew nearer to the light, proceeding with caution, they could see that it came from a camp-fire located near to a small group of trees standing to the left of it. They could see two men seated near the fire, not far from one tree which stood a little apart from the rest.

'Only two men,' said Jack. 'Seems like we're out of luck. But just in case they've split up let's take a closer look at them.'

They circled the group of trees and entered it at a point remote from the camp-fire. Cautiously, they made their way through the trees until they had a good view of the two men seated near the fire. They could now see that both men were complete strangers to them.

Jack was just about to signal to Ruth that they should both withdraw when he caught sight of something hanging from the branch of the tree which stood a little apart from the rest. Curious, he moved round to a point which gave him a better view of the tree. Ruth followed him. They were now close enough to see that a man was hanging from the tree. He was suspended on a rope attached to his wrists. His legs were tied together, his head was bare, and his feet were just clear of the ground.

As the body slowly revolved, swinging from side to side, Jack could see that the man was well-built, above average height, with long black shoulder-length hair and a black moustache. There was something familiar about him. When his face was briefly illuminated by a burst of flame from the fire, Jack recognized him. He was a deputy US marshal with whom he had worked many times in the past in the Indian Territory. He turned to Ruth.

'That's an old friend of mine hanging there,' he whispered. 'His name's Cal Archer. We worked together as lawmen for a long time. The two men near the fire must be criminals who've got the better of him. We've got to set him free.'

One of the men seated by the fire rose as Jack finished speaking and walked over to the prisoner. He looked at him for a moment, then called out to his partner. His words were clearly audible to Jack and Ruth.

'I don't see no point in Archer staying alive any longer,' he said. 'I reckon we could both do with a bit of target practice. Let's take a few shots at him, then we'll cut him down and leave him in the middle of those trees.'

The other man rose to his feet and walked up to his partner.

'A good idea,' he said. 'I'll take the head, you take the chest.'

As both men drew their sixguns, their attention was suddenly diverted from their prisoner by the sound of a shot, fired in the air, from Jack's gun.

They both turned, and saw Jack and Ruth run out of the trees towards them, holding their sixguns. The two men were both hit in the chest before they could take aim and fire. Both men dropped their guns and fell to the ground.

Jack walked up to them, kicked their weapons aside, and checked them over.

'They're both dead,' he said to Ruth. 'Let's take a look at Cal.'

They walked over to Archer and looked into his face. His eyes had opened at the sound of the shots and his head had lifted. Jack took his knife from his belt and sliced through the rope above Archer's wrists. Supporting his friend, he laid him on the ground and cut the rope around his legs. Concerned, he looked at Archer's bruised and battered face.

'Jack!' said Archer. 'I sure am glad to see you. I thought you were still in Colorado.'

'It's a long story,' said Jack. 'I'll tell you about it later. You look like you've been beaten up pretty bad. Is there anything broken?'

Archer sat up. 'I reckon not,' he said. 'Mainly stiff and sore. But you're forgetting your manners, Jack. Who's your friend?'

Jack introduced Ruth, then spoke to her about the shooting.

'We had no choice but to shoot at those two, Ruth,' he said, 'and we were lucky to get our shots in first. I was real glad to have you with me.'

Archer rose to his feet. 'It's a long time since I had anything to eat and drink,' he said. 'I'm going to see what these two men brought with them, and make myself a meal.'

'Let me help you,' said Ruth.

'I'll go and bring the horses here,' said Jack, 'and while I'm gone Ruth can tell you how we come to be here.'

When Jack returned they all had supper. During the meal Cal told the others how he had received a message from his mother asking him to return to the ranch in the Texas Panhandle where his father was seriously ill. He had been riding there in response to the message when he had been ambushed by the two men lying on the ground.

'I don't know them,' he said, 'but it turned out that the brother of one of them was an outlaw I shot dead during a bank-raid we'd got wind of in a town near the Texas border. So it was a matter of revenge.'

Jack gave Cal a detailed description of Craig and the men with him. He asked him if he had seen them recently.

'I sure have,' Cal replied. 'Not long before I was ambushed, I was in a town called Black Rock, about twenty miles south-east of here. I was just getting ready to leave my room at the hotel when I looked out of the window and saw three men riding into town.

'I took special notice because they had the look of criminals about them. But I didn't check up on them because I didn't recognize them and I was in a hurry to get to the ranch. I left town soon after.'

'It's good news for us, you seeing them,' said Jack. 'We lost their tracks a while back, and we ain't been able to pick them up since. We'll ride on to Black Rock. How about you?'

'I'll head for the ranch,' Cal replied. 'When you two get to Black Rock, will you send a message to Fort Smith, telling them what's happened here? And go and see Bell the liveryman. He's a friend of mine. He'll give you any help you need. He'll arrange for these two bodies to be picked up and maybe he'll have some more information for you about the three men you're after.'

They all rested a while and at dawn Jack and Ruth parted from Cal and headed for Black Rock. When they reached it they rode along the single street, lined with buildings on either side, and stopped outside the livery stable. Bell, the liveryman came out of the stable as they were dismounting.

Jack told him of the recent events involving Cal, and the reasons for the presence of Ruth and himself in the area. He passed on Cal's request about the recovery of the two bodies.

'I'll see to that,' said Bell. 'Is there anything else I can do for you?'

'The three men we're after,' said Jack. 'Like I said, Cal told me he'd seen them in Black Rock. Did you see them yourself?'

He went on to describe the three men.

'I sure did,' said Bell. 'They left their horses in the stable overnight. And I saw them in the saloon that evening, playing poker with a couple of men who live here in town.'

'Those two men,' asked Jack. 'Who are they?'

'They're called Price and Kenny,' Bell replied. 'They turned up here a couple of months ago and rented an empty shack on the edge of town. They're pretty close-mouthed. Nobody knows where they came from.'

'Did Craig and the other two seem friendly with them?' asked Jack.

'Not that I noticed,' Bell replied.

He went on to tell them that he had overhead Craig and one of his men talking outside the stable, and he got the impression that they were riding on to Cheriko, a town sixty miles or so to the east.

Kenny and Price happened to be in the store when Jack and Ruth stopped outside the livery stable. Kenny saw them through the window and looked at them closely while Price made some purchases. While Kenny was watching, Jack and Ruth walked off towards the hotel for a meal. Shortly after this Price and Kenny left the store and walked to their shack. Once inside, the two men who were, in fact, well acquainted with Craig, sat down to discuss a possible forthcoming operation for which he was offering them a large sum of money.

'There's no doubt,' said Kenny, 'that the man and woman who just rode into town are the ones Craig wants us to deal with. According to him he gave the liveryman the idea that he and the others were riding on to Cheriko. He reckoned this would be passed on to Tracy. So what we do is ride in that direction right now, find a good place for an ambush, and wait for them to come along.'

Five minutes later they departed.

Jack and Ruth left town an hour later, after sending a message to the US marshal in Fort Smith. Six miles out of town they came to a place where the trail passed through a group of large boulders. A man was walking towards them carrying a saddle on his shoulder. He stopped as they drew near, dropped the saddle on the ground, then sat down beside it.

'Somebody in trouble,' said Ruth, as the man waved to them.

When they reached him and dismounted, the man rose to his feet. But when he turned to face them they saw that there was a gun in his hand. Also, at that exact moment a second man, also holding a gun, ran out from behind a large boulder on the edge of the trail. It would have been futile for Jack and Ruth to resist. Their guns were taken and they stood side by side, faced by Kenny and Price.

'When Craig hired us to watch out for you two and take you prisoner if you turned up in Black Rock,' said Kenny, 'we never figured it'd be so easy. We're going to ride on for a spell to a place I know. Try to escape and we'll shoot you dead.'

The two prisoners were thoroughly searched, their hands were bound, and they were ordered to mount. Then Price collected his and Kenny's horses, which had been hidden from Jack and Ruth. The saddle was replaced and the four riders moved off to the east. After riding half a mile they branched to the right off the main trail and twenty minutes later came to a large hollow into which they rode. All four dismounted, close to a large cluster of rocks partially embedded in the ground. Kenny spoke to Jack.

'Craig's orders were,' he said, 'that one of you, and I'm talking about you Tracy, has got to die, but he don't want you to die quick. That's why we're here. I've been to this hollow before.'

'How about my partner?' asked Jack.

'It seems that Craig don't want her to die,' Kenny replied. 'He's got other plans for her. We're holding her till we hear from him. But we've got strict orders that the lady's not to be touched.'

He grinned at Ruth before turning again to Jack.

'We've thought up a good way to finish you off,' he said. 'A slow death, you could call it. Lie down on the ground.'

When Jack had done this Kenny checked the rope round his wrists and bound his legs together. Then, while Price kept hold of Ruth, Kenny dragged Jack a few yards to a hole in the ground. It was roughly circular, and about two feet in diameter at the surface.

'You can see that hole,' said Kenny to Jack. 'I looked down into it when we were last here, and after talking with Craig it seemed to us a good idea to bring you here. You'll see what I mean in a minute.'

He dragged Jack to a position where his feet were over the hole, lifted the upper part of his body, and dropped him through. As he disappeared from her view Jack heard Ruth's cry of despair.

As Jack's feet hit the floor of the underground cave he bent his knees, but was unable to prevent himself from falling forward. His head hit the hard floor. Momentarily stunned, he lay on the floor. When he recovered, he rolled over and looked up at the entrance above. There was no indication that Ruth and the two men were still there.

As far as he could tell his body had suffered no serious damage during the fall. Looking around, he could see that the floor of the cave was circular, with a diameter of ten feet or so. The wall was vertical and at no point less than ten feet high. The hole in the roof was directly over the centre of the floor. From what he could see, it looked as though escape from the cave, unaided, was impossible through the hole by which he had entered.

He turned himself to the task of freeing his arms and legs. He squirmed his way around through the debris on the floor of the cave until he found what he was looking for — a firm projecting sharp-edged piece of rock near the foot of the wall.

He positioned himself so that he was able to rub the rope holding his hands together against the sharp edge of the piece of rock. It was a slow and laborious process, but eventually the rope parted and he was able to remove the rope from around his legs. He stood upright and flexed his legs. Looking upwards, he could see that night was falling. By the time he had explored the cave, and had come to the conclusion that escape through the entrance above was impossible without outside help, it was dark.

He sat on the floor with his back to the wall. His thoughts turned to Ruth. He could imagine her feelings of utter despair and apprehension about the future. He lay down on the floor, where he spent a restless night.

At dawn he rose to his feet and examined the cave, more closely this time. On the previous day he had noticed a trickle of water running across the floor of the cave, and had used this to quench his thirst. Investigating further, he saw that the water was leaving the cave through a crack at the foot of the wall. Then he found the point of entry. The water was trickling from the bottom of a hole, about twelve inches in diameter, at the foot of the wall.

He knelt down, extended one arm into the hole, and discovered that after just an inch or two it widened considerably. He found a suitable piece of rock on the floor, and with it he enlarged the hole until it was wide enough for him to pass through. Beyond the entrance he could see a passage just large enough to allow him to move along it in a lying position. He decided to investigate. Perhaps he would find another exit from the cave.

He crawled through the hole into the passage with his arms extended in front of him and inched his way forward. His progress was slow and it was too dark for him to see what lay ahead. As he progressed he could feel that the passage was gradually getting smaller. He had covered a distance of fifteen yards when his outstretched hand met an obstacle in front of him and he could feel that the passage was firmly blocked. He had no option but to return to the cave.

He rested for a while, then started to inch his way backwards. But he had not progressed more than a few feet when he felt a sudden pressure on his back and shoulders, and realized that the roof of the passage had caved in on him. Fighting back a rising sense of panic, he redoubled his efforts to propel himself backwards. But gradually his movement was more and more restricted and eventually he found himself firmly jammed in the passage, with no means of freeing himself, and the prospect of a slow lingering death ahead of him.

6

When Jack had been dropped into the underground cave Ruth was taken to the horses which were standing nearby. The saddles and bridles were taken off the horses which had been ridden by herself and Jack, and were hidden in a patch of brush. Ruth was ordered on to Price's mount and they rode out of the hollow, Price riding double with Kenny and leading the two unsaddled horses, which were turned loose soon after they left the hollow. They headed for Black Rock, Kenny setting a pace which would bring them there after dark.

As they rode along, Ruth assessed the situation in her mind. She had no idea of how far Jack had fallen when he was dropped into the hole and how badly injured he might be. She was determined to seize the slightest opportunity to break free and go to his assistance.

It was dark when they approached Black Rock and they reached the shack without being observed. Ruth had been gagged before they reached town. Inside the shack she was ordered to sit on the floor with her back to the wall, and her legs were bound.

Later in the evening, after they had all taken food and drink, Price and Kenny lay down on two bunks, leaving an oil-lamp burning, with the wick turned down low. Ruth was in view of both men. Kenny was asleep almost immediately, but for some time Ruth was conscious that Price was staring at her. Then he too fell asleep.

She had been gagged, her hands and feet were bound, and to prevent her from moving around the shack she was roped to a stout hook that had been screwed into the wall behind her. Her hands were slim and she thought it might be possible to slip them out from the rope which was binding them together. After some time and effort she had managed to loosen the rope a little, but not sufficiently to allow her to free her hands. Exhausted, she was obliged to abandon the attempt and she rested fitfully for the rest of the night.

It was around half past eight when both men woke and Kenny left his bunk. Both men ignored Ruth.

'We'll have breakfast later,' said Kenny. 'We've got to get that message to Craig. I'll write it out now and take it to the telegraph office.'

He busied himself with pencil and paper for a while, then left the shack. Price left his bunk a few minutes after Kenny had departed. He glanced at Ruth. The ropes holding her appeared to be secure.

'I'm going outside for a few minutes,' he said. 'No point you trying to get loose. Give us any trouble and we're liable to forget what Craig said.'

Grinning at her, he left the shack, closing the door behind him.

Forcing herself to stay calm, Ruth renewed her efforts to release her hands. Exerting all her strength, and breaking the skin on her hands in the process, she forced them free. Quickly, she freed her legs and removed the rope tying her to the wall. She removed the gag and rose to her feet. Desperately, she looked around for a weapon, but none was visible, even though she had seen Kenny carry into the shack the weapons taken from herself and Jack.

She had just embarked on a frantic search for a weapon when she heard a noise outside the door. She ran over to the stove, picked up a large, heavy frying-pan and ran to stand against the wall by the door. A moment later the door opened and Price stepped inside. He glanced towards the corner where Ruth had been sitting. At the same instant that he realized she was not there Ruth stepped out from behind the door and struck him hard on the side of his head with the bottom of the pan. Stunned, he collapsed on the floor.

Ruth took Price's gun from its holster, then ran over to the window facing on to the street. There was no sign of Kenny. She quickly gagged Price, bound him hand and foot, and dragged him out of sight between the two bunks. She ran back to the window. She could see Kenny approaching. In half a minute he would be at the door.

Encouraged by her previous success with the frying-pan Ruth picked it up again and stood by the door. But Kenny's reaction was quicker than that of his partner. On opening the door he immediately sensed that something was wrong. He pushed the door to behind him, stepped away from Ruth, and started turning to face her. At the same time he went for his gun. Ruth dropped the pan, beat him to the draw, and sent a bullet into his right arm. His gun dropped to the floor and he stumbled backwards a couple of paces. Keeping him covered, Ruth picked up his gun with her left hand, then ordered him to sit in a corner of the shack. When he had complied, she walked into the doorway and fired five equally spaced shots from Kenny's gun into the air.

The sound of the gunfire did not go unnoticed. It prompted three townsmen to hurry along the street towards the shack. Seeing Ruth in the doorway with a gun in her hand, they stopped short. One of the three was Bell the liveryman. Ruth called out to him.

'Will you come up close, Mr Bell?' she asked.

The liveryman walked up to her and, still keeping Kenny covered, she explained the situation to him.

'I've got to go and help Jack,' she said. 'I'm praying he's still alive. Can you see that these two men in here are held prisoner until the law can pick them up? My guess is that they're outlaws.'

'I can arrange that,' said Bell, 'and then me and you and a friend of mine will go and see if we can help your partner.'

He walked into the shack and looked at Kenny and Price. At Ruth's request he looked for the weapons belonging to Ruth and Jack, and found them under one of the bunks. He called to the two men outside to come in. He explained the situation and asked them to guard the two men for the time being.

Then he took Ruth along to his house and left her in the care of his wife while he arranged for the prisoners to be guarded until they were picked up, and for the doctor to tend to Kenny's wounds. Lastly, before returning to his house he went to see his friend Ed Foster the blacksmith.

Back at his house, he told Ruth that Foster would be coming with them to the hollow, and that he was working on a crude rope-ladder which they could use to get in and out of the cave. It would be ready in half an hour.

They left Black Rock forty minutes later, leading a spare saddled horse, and carrying the rope-ladder, some extra rope, and two oil-lamps. When they neared the hollow Ruth rode in front and led them to the cave entrance. The two men anchored the top of the ladder to a nearby rock and Bell climbed down it into the cave, followed by Ruth. Foster lowered two oil-lamps down to them.

Ruth and Bell examined the cave and soon found, lying on the floor, the rope which had secured Jack's hands and legs. But there was no sign of Jack himself.

'He's managed to free himself,' said Ruth, 'but where has he gone? He couldn't possibly get out through that hole up there without help.'

She looked around the cave again and noticed the hole at the foot of the wall. She and Bell walked over to it and observed the debris left on the floor when Jack had enlarged the hole. By the light of an oil-lamp they were able to see the passage behind it.

'That's where he's gone,' said Ruth. 'He was looking for another way out. I've got to go in there and see what's happened. It's clear I'm the best one for the job. It's a narrow passage and I'm a lot slimmer than you or your friend.'

Bell could see that Ruth was

adamant. He called out to Foster above. He told him what they had found and asked him to throw some rope down. Ruth grasped the small loop at the end of the rope in one hand. Then she lay down and shouted Jack's name into the hole several times. There was no response. She spoke to Bell.

'I'll go in now,' she said. 'I'll pull this rope through with me. It'll give you some idea how far I've gone in. If I find Jack I'll give three jerks on the rope.'

Lying flat, face down, she entered the hole and worked her way along the passage, pushing the lamp in front of her. Progress seemed slow and she rested from time to time. Then, a little way ahead of her she could see what looked like a blockage of the tunnel. She redoubled her efforts. When she eventually pushed the lamp up against the blockage she could clearly see the soles of a pair of boots protruding from it.

Her heart sank. Could Jack possibly still be alive? She caught hold of the sole of one boot and twisted it from side to side. The response was almost immediate. The two boots moved in unison. She gave three sharp pulls on the rope, then closely examined the roof fall which had imprisoned Jack. She removed the debris around his feet and tied the rope around his ankles. Then, leaving the lamp where it was, she slowly backed down the passage and into the cave.

She told Bell what she had found.

'I'm going back in there,' she said. 'I'm going to clear away as much rubble as I can from around Jack's body. When I've done that I reckon you might be able to pull him clear of the roof fall. Then maybe he'll be able to back out of the passage himself.'

'Let me know when you want me to start pulling,' said Bell, 'and we'd better decide on signals on the rope for pulling and not pulling.'

When these had been agreed Ruth worked her way along the passage back to Jack. She removed as much of the loose debris around his body as she could, then signalled to Bell to pull. The liveryman braced his feet on the two sides of the hole and gradually increased the pull on the rope. Suddenly, Jack's body moved towards Ruth a couple of inches, then stopped as more loose material fell down from the roof.

Ruth signalled to Bell to stop pulling, then removed the material and signalled to the liveryman to start pulling again. This time, Jack's body moved more easily, and slowly Bell pulled him clear of the fall. Ruth signalled him to stop pulling and called out to Jack.

'Are you all right, Jack?' she asked.

'I'm all right,' he replied. 'A few cuts and bruises is all. But I couldn't move. Until I felt you move my boot, I thought I was a goner.'

After checking with Jack that he could back out into the cave himself, Ruth removed the rope from his feet and together they moved along the passage and into the cave. As Bell helped Jack to his feet they heard a loud rumble coming from the passage which Jack and Ruth had just vacated.

'Sounds like you both got out just in time,' said Bell.

Fifteen minutes later they were riding out of the hollow on their way to Black Rock. As they rode along Ruth told Jack how she had escaped from her captors, who were now being held prisoner in Black Rock. She told him of the telegraph message which Denny had sent to Craig.

When they rode into town Jack thanked Bell and Foster for their help. He said that he and Ruth would be taking rooms at the hotel and he asked Bell if it would be possible for him to see the telegraph message which had gone to Craig.

'That shouldn't be a problem,' said the liveryman. 'Kenny's a criminal. I know the operator well. I'll go along there now and get a copy. I'll bring it to the hotel.'

Jack thanked Bell and he and Ruth

went on to the hotel. The liveryman came to see them twenty minutes later, with a copy of the message. It read:

ABE WILSON LATIGO INDIAN TER-RITORY.

JOB DONE. HOLDING PACKAGE FOR YOU. WHERE AND WHEN DO I DELIVER. PRICE WILL NOT BE WITH ME. REPLY TO ME AT BLACK ROCK. KENNY.

'This Abe Wilson,' said Jack. 'Either he's working for Craig or one of the gang is using the name as an alias. And Craig must be hiding out somewhere near Latigo. I think that's about fifty miles south-east of here.'

'That's right,' said Bell.

'We'd better wait here till a reply comes to Denny's message,' said Jack.

'I'll ask the telegraph operator to bring it to you as soon as he gets it,' said Bell.

The reply to the message was

brought to Jack and Ruth at the hotel two days later, just after noon. The day was Tuesday. The message read:

DELIVER PACKAGE TO S AND C NOON THURSDAY AT INDIAN BLUFF SOUTH OF LATIGO. WILSON.

'So forty-eight hours from now,' said Jack, 'Craig will be expecting you and Kenny to turn up at Indian Bluff. I suppose 'C' and 'S' stand for Carney and Slater. So they'll be there, expecting to take you over from Kenny. I reckon if we could take them by surprise we could get the better of those two. What d'you think?'

'A good idea,' said Ruth. 'What's your plan?'

When they had settled on a plan they went to see Bell, showed him the telegraph message, and told him of their plan to confront Slater and Carney.

'I have a brother Frank in Latigo,'

said Bell. 'He runs the general store there. Maybe he can help you. I'll give you a letter for him.'

'We're obliged,' said Jack. 'We'll be riding to Latigo tomorrow. If the deputy marshals haven't turned up before we leave, will you tell them that we've gone to Indian Bluff?'

'I'll do that,' said Bell.

'One other thing,' said Jack. 'Does Kenny always wear that black shirt and vest, and that black Montana Peak hat?'

'I've never seen him in anything else,' Bell replied.

The following day Jack and Ruth rode to Latigo. They timed their journey so as to arrive after nightfall. They rode up to the store, to find it closed. They walked round to the door of the house at the rear. Frank Bell answered their knock and Jack gave him the letter from his brother. He invited them into the living-room, where his wife was seated. Jack explained the situation to them, then asked about Indian Bluff. Bell told them it was six miles south of Latigo. From the top of the bluff, riders approaching from any direction could be seen well before they reached it.

Jack asked whether there was somewhere, not too far from the bluff, where they could watch it through field glasses from cover.

'There's a small flat-topped hill this side of the bluff with some trees at the foot,' said Bell. 'That should do.'

Jack said he would like to hire some clothing for a short spell and Bell took him into the store. When they returned to the house Jack was carrying a black vest and shirt, and a black Montana Peak hat.

'We'd like a few words with the telegraph operator,' said Jack, 'concerning a couple of telegraph messages.'

'I'll take you to see him now,' said Bell. 'I expect he's still in his office.'

Jack showed the operator the copies of the telegraph messages sent and received by Kenny.

'The same man picked up the

message and sent the reply,' said the operator. 'He was a stranger to me. I'd never seen him in town before.'

At Jack's request he described the man.

'That's Craig, for sure,' said Jack. 'The gang must have been hiding out somewhere nearby.'

Jack and Ruth thanked the operator and Bell and went to the hotel, where they took two rooms.

7

Jack and Ruth rose in time to allow them to reach before daybreak the flat-topped hill described by the store-keeper. They left their horses hidden in the trees and climbed to the top of the hill. Jack was wearing the black clothing supplied by Bell. They sat on the ground, waiting for the dawn.

'We should be able to get pretty close to them, Ruth,' said Jack, 'before they realize I'm not Kenny. It's lucky I'm about the same build as him. But don't forget what dangerous killers these two are. If there's any gunplay, shoot to kill.'

When the sun rose Indian Bluff was clearly visible. The sheer side of the bluff was facing them. They both lay down and took turns looking through the glasses for riders heading for the bluff. It was just before ten o'clock when Ruth saw two riders moving in that direction. She handed the glasses to Jack, who studied the two riders intently.

'I'm pretty sure that they're Slater and Carney,' he said.

As Jack watched, the two riders disappeared behind the bluff, to reappear twenty-five minutes later, walking along the top. Then they sank down out of sight.

Jack and Ruth waited a further forty minutes, then crawled off the top of the hill and went for their horses. When they rode out from behind the hill and headed for the bluff, Jack was leading Ruth's horse and Ruth was riding with her hands behind her. In her right hand she was holding her Colt Peacemaker.

As they neared the bluff they saw the two men who had been hiding on top rise to their feet and disappear down the sloping south side. Jack and Ruth rode to within twenty yards of the bluff and stopped. The two men were not yet in sight. They both dismounted and Ruth tucked her sixgun under the back of her belt. They stood waiting until Slater and Carney appeared, having walked around the foot of the bluff.

The outlaws came to a halt as Jack and Ruth started walking towards them.

Ruth was walking in front with her hands raised. Jack walked close behind her with his sixgun in his hand. Twelve yards from the two outlaws Ruth stopped and drew her sixgun. At the same time Jack stepped out and moved up beside her. He called out to the two men in front of him.

'Hands up!' he shouted. 'Make a move for your guns and you're both dead.'

Badly shocked by the totally unexpected appearance of Jack, the outlaws hesitated briefly. Then each of them went for his gun. Before they could pull the triggers Ruth and Jack had fired and both outlaws went down. Still holding his gun Jack walked up to them. He checked each man, then turned to Ruth.

'They had their chance to face a trial,' he said. 'But they didn't take it. They're both dead. We'll take their bodies back to Latigo with us.'

He went to find the outlaws' horses and when he returned he and Ruth looked through the dead men's pockets and saddle-bags to see if they could find anything which would help them locate Craig. But the search proved unsuccessful.

Jack lifted the two bodies on to the outlaws' horses and they headed for Latigo. When they reached town they stopped outside the store. Bell saw them through the window. Leaving his wife in charge, he went outside. A small group collected, looking at the bodies.

'These two men,' said Jack, 'are called Slater and Carney. They're members of the Laredo gang. Can the undertaker take care of them?'

One of the onlookers stepped forward. 'I'm the undertaker,' he said. 'I'll see to it.'

'Right,' said Jack. 'Take the bodies.

I'll call in to see you later.'

Bell took Jack and Ruth into his living-room, where they told him what had happened at Indian Bluff.

'I sure am glad to see you both back alive,' said the storekeeper. 'What're you aiming to do now?'

'We've been talking about that,' Jack replied. 'We've no idea where Craig might be. We think our best plan is to backtrack Slater and Carney from the bluff. Maybe that'll lead us to Craig. But we need a good tracker for that. Is there anybody around here we might be able to hire?'

'Only one man,' Bell replied, 'and that's Tom Veale. For a long time he served as a scout in the cavalry. He retired a few months back and came to live here, near his son. I'll take you to see him.'

They found Veale in his small house along the street. He invited them inside. He was a sturdy, weatherbeaten man in his sixties, still keen of eye. Jack told him that they wanted to hire an expert tracker for a short while, and he explained why.

'To tell the truth,' said Veale, 'I'm a mite tired of just sitting around remembering all the things I used to do. I reckon a bit of excitement wouldn't do me no harm. When do we leave?'

'At daybreak tomorrow,' said Jack. 'But we didn't figure on you taking a hand in any gunplay. All we want from you is to help us get some idea of where Craig might be.'

At daybreak, Jack and Ruth picked up Veale at his house and they rode to Indian Bluff. Veale soon found the tracks of the horses which had been ridden by Slater and Carney the previous day. Riding ahead of Jack and Ruth he followed the tracks eastward. The two riders behind him were impressed by his skill in following tracks which were largely invisible to them.

They had travelled a little over eight miles from the bluff when Veale raised his arm for them to stop. He dismounted, studied the ground for a while, then walked a short distance towards the south-west before beckoning them to join him.

'Up to this point,' he told them, 'there were three riders. Then one of them left the other two and headed south-west.'

'There's a good chance that that rider was Craig,' said Jack. 'Let's follow him.'

After they had ridden about ten miles they were hit by a torrential rainstorm moving slowly in a north-easterly direction. When it eventually stopped raining Veale spoke to his companions.

'I'm sorry,' he said. 'I can help you no more. That rain's washed out all the tracks. But just over that ridge ahead is Clanton. Likely Craig was heading there. I sure hope you get news of him when you ride into town. As for me, I'll ride back to Black Rock. I'm beginning to realize I ain't as spry as I used to be.'

Jack and Ruth thanked Veale for his

help and paid him for his time. Then they parted company with him and rode on to Clanton. Riding first to the livery stable they had a conversation with the liveryman. He told them that a man answering Craig's description had called at the stable the previous day, during the afternoon, and had left the horse at the stable for feed and water.

'He picked the horse up this morning,' the liveryman went on, 'and he rode out of town to the south. When he was leaving, I asked him, casual-like, where he was going, but he told me that was his business. He sure had a mean look about him.'

'What's the next place south of here?' asked Jack.

'That's Tresco,' replied the liveryman. 'It's about forty-five miles from here.'

They thanked the liveryman and went to the restaurant over the street to take a meal. Over it they discussed their next move.

'There's a few hours daylight left,

Ruth,' said Jack. 'As soon as we've eaten I think we should follow Craig south.'

Ruth agreed and they left town as soon as the meal was over.

* * *

On the previous day, when Craig left his horse at the livery stable, he went to the saloon. Massiter, the owner of the saloon, took him to a private room behind the bar. Massiter, an old acquaintance of Craig, was well known to criminals who were seeking refuge in the Indian Territory from lawmen who wanted them for crimes committed in the surrounding states. Ostensibly just a saloon-owner, Massiter ran a lucrative business directing criminals to safe hideouts in the Indian Territory.

'I'm here,' said Craig, 'because I've lost Chandler and I want somebody to take his place. And on top of that I'm thinking of taking on another man to bring us up to five. I've heard that Rooney and Vickery are in this area. I'd like to proposition them. D'you know where they are?'

'It so happens I do,' Massiter replied, 'and I reckon they'd jump at the chance of joining the Laredo gang. They ain't been doing too well lately. They bungled their last job in Texas and very nearly got caught They're hiding out in a ravine a little way off the trail six miles south of here.'

'I'll ride out there tomorrow morning,' said Craig. 'I'll talk things over with Rooney and Vickery. I'll ride back here in the evening to let you know what's happened. After that I'm going to join up with Slater and Carney. They'll be waiting for me at a spot not far from here.'

'All right,' said Massiter, and he told Craig exactly where the hideout of Rooney and Vickery was located.

'When you get near,' he said, 'tie a bandanna on your rifle barrel and hold it up in the air. Otherwise you're liable to get shot.'

Craig rode out of town the following

morning. He found both the outlaws at the ravine and discussed with them the possibility of their joining the gang. The two men both welcomed the suggestion. Craig decided to return to Clanton that evening, and on the following day to bring Slater and Carney to the ravine to join up with the new members of the gang.

* * *

On the day of Craig's visit to Vickery and Rooney, Massiter was standing behind the saloon bar in Clanton, in the late afternoon, listening idly to a conversation between two men standing on the other side of the bar. One, who had just arrived from Black Rock, was a stranger to him. The other was the liveryman.

Massiter pricked up his ears as he heard the Laredo gang mentioned. He listened intently as the stranger told how two of the gang had been killed at Indian Bluff, near Black Rock, by a man called Tracy and a woman called Mailer who was riding with him. The stranger said that the couple were now on the trail of a man called Craig, who was the leader of the gang.

'I'm sure that Tracy and his partner were here a few hours ago,' said the liveryman. 'They were asking me if I'd seen a man who must have been Craig. I told them he'd left town this morning, heading south.'

Massiter told the barkeep that he was leaving the saloon for a while. Then he went for his horse and rode out of town to the south. He had ridden a couple of miles, and nightfall was not far away, when he saw Craig approaching him. When they met, Massiter told Craig about the killing of his men by Jack and Ruth. He also told him that it was known by Tracy and his partner that Craig himself had been in Clanton overnight and had ridden off to the south that morning.

'I reckon they headed south after you,' Massiter said, 'and likely they'll end up in Tresco.'

'Damnation!' said Craig, his face flushed with rage. 'I've got to get rid of those two. I'll ride back to the ravine, then all three of us will go after Tracy and his partner. A good place to start might be Tresco. I'm obliged to you for letting me know about this.'

The two men parted and Massiter rode back to town.

★　★　★

During their ride to Tresco, all enquiries by Jack and Ruth as to whether anyone had seen Craig, proved fruitless. The same applied when they reached the town. They decided to stay there until the following day, in case he turned up.

'I could do with a good night's sleep,' said Ruth.

They took two rooms at the hotel. From Jack's room, except when they were taking a meal, they kept watch on the street outside. Just before dark they saw two riders arrive in town from the north. The riders dismounted and passed out of view into the hotel. Both were strangers to the couple watching them.

Quickly, Jack left the room and moved to the top of the stairs leading down to the lobby. Peering around the corner he could see the two men standing at the desk with their backs to him. They were alone. One of them turned round the register which Jack and Ruth had signed earlier and drew his companion's attention to something on the page. He turned the register back and rang the bell on the desk. The owner appeared and Jack heard the man asking for two rooms for the night. Jack returned to Ruth. They saw the two men take their horses to the livery stable, then return to the hotel. They heard them walking along the passage outside and entering their rooms. Jack told Ruth what he had seen in the lobby.

'I didn't like the look of those two,'

he said. 'It could be that Craig knows about us killing Slater and Carney, and he's sent these two to get rid of us. I think we'd better get ready for them, just in case they try something during the night.'

He walked over to the door and inspected it closely. The only means of gaining some privacy was by using a very flimsy bolt on the inside of the door. Jack could see that very little effort would be needed to burst it open from the outside.

He walked back to the bed, and with Ruth's help he lifted the mattress off the solid piece of timber on which it was resting, and placed it on the floor between the bed and the window. Then, using a spare blanket and pillow from the wardrobe, they produced a fair imitation of a body lying on the bed underneath a blanket.

'I reckon that could fool anybody in the dark,' said Jack. 'Let's do the same thing in your room.'

When they had done this, they

returned to Jack's room. They heard the two men leave their rooms and return an hour later. Soon after this, Ruth went to her room, bolted the door, and lay on the mattress. Her sixgun was lying on the floor close by. In a few minutes she was asleep. Jack sat in a chair for a while, then he too lay down with a sixgun by his side.

Both of them were rudely awakened just after one o'clock in the morning, when the doors of their rooms were burst open at exactly the same moment. A lamp at the top of the stairs lightened the darkness very slightly in the two rooms, and Vickery and Rooney could see well enough to empty their guns into what they thought were the bodies of their intended victims.

Ruth and Jack both stayed down until the gunfire had ceased and the two intruders had turned and started running out of the rooms. Then they rose above the bed in time to fire only one shot before the intruders had disappeared from the rooms, to head downstairs and out to the two horses which had been brought from the livery stable earlier and were waiting outside.

Jack checked that Ruth was all right, then opened her window and looked out. He could hear the sound of horses riding fast out of town. He closed the window and lit the lamp on the table.

'I'm pretty sure I hit one of them,' said Ruth, 'but just where I hit him, I don't know.'

'I think I hit one as well,' said Jack, 'probably in the back of the right shoulder.'

A moment later, Bond, the hotel owner, woken by the sound of gunfire, turned up to investigate. Jack told him what had happened. Bond inspected the damage in both rooms.

'I'll have this put right later,' he said. 'Meanwhile you can have two of the other rooms for the rest of the night.'

Over an early breakfast Jack discussed the situation with Ruth.

'Bond's just told me,' he said, 'that he found a trail of blood-spots along the passage, down the stairs and out into the street. So at least one of them is injured. And I'm sure I sent a bullet into the back of one of them. I think they'll be needing help from a doctor.

'Bond tells me that, apart from the doctor here in town, the nearest one by far is at Listow, twenty miles south of here. Maybe that's where they'll go. And maybe Craig'll be with them. I think we should head for Listow right after breakfast.'

'I can't think of any better idea,' said Ruth.

8

When Vickery and Rooney rejoined Craig at the spot where he had made camp two miles east of town, he listened with mounting anger and frustration as they told him of the failed attempt on the couple who had been involved in the deaths of three members of his gang.

Vickery and Rooney were both injured. A bullet from Ruth's sixgun had severely gouged the back of Vickery's left hand, and it had been bleeding profusely. Rooney had a bullet wound in the back of his right shoulder. Craig put some temporary bandaging on the wounds.

'I've got to get rid of those two once and for all,' he said. 'I think I'd better put Snyder on the job. Have you heard of him?'

'I have,' said Vickery. 'They say that if

Snyder is out to kill you, you're as good as dead.'

'That's right,' said Craig, 'and he's not the sort of gunslinger that shoots it out with you face to face. He favours the shot in the back, on a dark night.'

'Can you get hold of him?' asked Vickery.

'There's a chance he may be hiding out at Parker's store,' Craig replied. 'He often stays there between jobs. The store's less than twenty miles from here.'

'That can wait,' said Rooney. 'I've got to see a doctor. This bullet's got to be taken out of my back. I know there's a doctor in Listow. We need to get there as quick as we can.'

'No need for that,' said Craig. 'Parker has a man working for him who spent a few years helping an army doctor. He'll take the bullet out for you. And Parker's place is a lot nearer than Listow. If we leave here now we should get there before dawn.'

They arrived at Parker's store just as

the sun was rising. Craig hammered on the door, which was locked. It was opened by Parker, a short, middle-aged man who, recognizing Craig, invited them inside and closed and fastened the door behind them.

'Both of these men with me have been shot,' said Craig. 'Can Pardoe take a look at them?'

'Sure,' said Parker. 'Wait here.'

He returned soon after with Pardoe, a thick-set swarthy man who took a quick look at the wounds. Then he led the two injured men through a door at the rear of the store.

'He'll fix them up,' said Parker to Craig.

'Can we stay here till the wounds heal?' asked Craig.

'It so happens I have three spare rooms,' said Parker. 'Payment in advance, as usual.'

'All right,' said Craig. 'We'll take them. And while we're here I want to contact Snyder. D'you know where he is?'

'You're in luck,' said Parker. 'He rode in two days ago. Said he'd be here about a week. He'll be taking breakfast in the dining-room before long. Listen for the bell.'

'That's good news,' said Craig. 'I'll see him there. I have a job for him if he'll take it. Meanwhile, can I see how Vickery and Rooney are doing?'

Parker took him through a door at the rear of the store which led into a large timber structure which contained a kitchen, living-room, dining-room, and eight small rooms normally used as bedrooms. In one of these Pardoe was attending to the two injured men, using a small selection of surgical instruments.

Craig watched as Pardoe removed the bullet from Rooney's shoulder, then treated the wound on the back of Vickery's hand. When he had finished bandaging the wounds, he spoke to the two injured men.

'Those wounds should heal up all right,' he said, 'but the days when you can handle a right-hand sixgun are over. I'm advising both of you to start to practise using a left-hand gun.'

Pardoe showed the three of them to their rooms. When Craig went to the dining-room for breakfast he found Snyder sitting at a small table on his own. Snyder's appearance gave no hint of his reputation as a cold ruthless killer. He was a short, jovial-looking man with side-whiskers, running slightly to fat. He beckoned Craig into the seat opposite him.

'Parker tells me you have a proposition for me,' he said.

'That's right,' said Craig, and went on to explain the situation.

'I can see why you want to get rid of those two,' said Snyder, 'but it ain't going to be cheap. I've got two people to deal with, and they're not exactly amateurs when it comes to handling a gun.'

'You can name your price,' said Craig.

'In that case,' said Snyder, 'I'll leave

for Tresco right after breakfast. Maybe they're still there. If not, maybe I can find out where they've gone. How long are you staying here?'

'Only until both Vickery and Rooney are fit to ride,' said Craig.

'Maybe I'll be back before you leave,' said Snyder. 'If not, you can take it for granted those two won't bother you again.'

★ ★ ★

When Snyder reached Tresco he went straight to the saloon, usually an excellent source of information. He went up to the bar and ordered a beer. It was not long before he had the full story of two guests being attacked at the hotel during the night by two men who had escaped. Also, he was told that the two hotel guests, a man and a woman, had left town only a few hours earlier, heading for Listow. They thought that the two men who had been shot at might have gone to the doctor there.

Snyder went for a meal in the hotel, then rode off towards Listow. It was a hot day, and during the journey he looked for a place where he could water his horse. Seeing a ravine a little way off the trail, he rode over to it, but there was no stream running through. He noticed an old cabin in the ravine. Curious, he rode up to it, and looked inside. It was obvious that it had not been occupied for a long time. He resumed his journey towards Listow. As he rode along, his mind was working on a plan which, provided that he found his quarry in Listow, could bring his current mission to a successful conclusion.

He arrived at Listow during the evening, and went straight to the hotel. Inside, he asked Kelly, the hotel manager, whether a man called Tracy had arrived there, with a woman companion, earlier in the day.

'They sure did,' replied Kelly. 'They're staying here.'

'My name's Allison,' said Snyder. 'I

need to have a word with them. D'you know where they are?'

'In the dining-room,' Kelly replied. 'I'll take you there.'

He led Snyder into the dining-room, where Jack and Ruth were sitting at a table just finishing a meal. Earlier, they had spoken with the doctor, who had received no visit from Vickery and Rooney. They had decided to stay the night at Listow.

Kelly pointed the couple out to Snyder and left. Snyder walked up to the table and stood there, beaming down on Jack and Ruth.

'My name's Allison,' he said. 'I have some information that might be useful to you.'

Jack motioned to the spare chair at the table and Snyder sat down.

'I run a freight company in Texas,' he said, 'and I'm thinking of expanding operations into the Indian Territory. I've been riding around the territory to see how much business I might be able to pick up.'

'I've seen your freight wagons all over the Texas Panhandle,' said Jack, 'and I know you have a good reputation there. I reckon you'd do well in the territory.'

'That's what I feel now,' said Snyder. 'But that's not what I wanted to talk to you about. I rode into Tresco this morning, on my way to Listow, just after you'd left for Listow yourselves. They were all talking about what happened at the hotel, and about you leaving for Listow after the men who tried to kill you.'

He went on to tell how, on his way to Listow, he had been looking for a place to water his horse when he came across an old tumbledown cabin in a secluded ravine. Inside the cabin he had noticed some bloodstains on the floor which looked quite fresh. Also on the floor were a bloodstained bandanna and a torn-off part of a shirt.

'I didn't think a lot of it at the time,' he went on, 'but then I remembered about you firing at the two men in the hotel, and I wondered if they had been in the cabin.'

'That's very interesting,' said Jack. 'D'you remember anything particular about the bandanna or the shirt?'

It so happened that Snyder had seen Rooney and Vickery when Pardoe had led them out of the store for treatment, earlier that day.

'They were badly bloodstained,' he replied, 'but I'm sure it was a light-coloured spotted bandanna. Can't tell you anything about the shirt.'

'One of the men was wearing a bandanna like that,' said Jack. 'How far away is this ravine?'

'About six miles, I reckon,' said Snyder. 'I'll take you there tomorrow morning if you like. I've got a few hours to spare.'

'If they've been there, maybe we can pick up their trail at the cabin,' said Jack. 'We'd be obliged if you'd lead us there.'

The following morning Snyder led Jack and Ruth to the cabin. They dismounted outside it, and Snyder held back as they approached the door. Jack entered first, followed by Ruth, and they looked round for the bloodstains and the pieces of clothing.

Snyder entered close behind Ruth, drawing his sixgun from a concealed holster inside his jacket. He lifted Ruth's sixgun from its holster and threw it into a corner. Then he clamped his left arm around Ruth's neck and held the barrel of his cocked gun against the side of her head. Jack swung round, his hand reaching for his sixgun.

'Draw that and the lady's dead,' shouted Snyder.

Jack's hand moved away from the holster.

'The reason I didn't make it simple and shoot you both in the back,' said Snyder, 'is because Craig wanted me to let you know, before you died, that he'd hired me for the job of killing you.'

Snyder ordered Jack to lift his gun

out of the holster with his thumb and finger and drop it on the floor. As Jack's hand moved towards his gun Ruth, in desperation, punched upwards with her right fist, knocking the barrel of the gun away from her head. Immediately following this, she ducked her head and kicked Snyder hard on the shin with the heel of her boot. Then she dropped to the floor.

Snyder's gun went off, but the bullet embedded itself harmlessly in the wall. He turned towards Jack, recocking his gun. But he was too late. Jack's shot hit him in the chest before he could fire. The shot was lethal. Snyder staggered back against the wall, then collapsed on the floor. Jack picked up his gun, then checked that he was dead. He turned to Ruth, who, shaking a little, had risen to her feet.

'That was a close call, Ruth,' he said. 'I reckon you saved both our lives. This man sure fooled us. I wonder who he really is?'

He went through the dead man's

pockets, but found no clue as to his real identity. In the man's saddle-bags he found only a box of expensive-looking big cigars of a type he had not seen in the territory before.

'Wonder where he got those,' he said. 'We'd better take the body back to Listow. Kelly told me that a couple of deputy US marshals might be calling there today. Maybe they'll be there when we get back.'

They hoisted the body on to the back of the dead man's horse and rode towards Listow. They were halfway there when they became aware of two riders coming up behind them. They halted and awaited their arrival. Jack recognized one of them as deputy Phil Lawton, with whom he had ridden on a number of operations in the territory. The recognition was mutual.

'Jack!' said Lawton, looking at the body on the horse. 'We heard that you two were in the territory, chasing the Laredo gang. Meet my partner Bill Kilroy.'

They all dismounted and Jack introduced Ruth, then explained the presence of the dead body.

'This man was hired by Craig to kill us,' said Jack, 'but I've no idea who he is. Have you seen him before?'

Both deputies took a look at Snyder's face.

'That's Snyder,' said Lawton. 'I saw his face on a poster a couple of weeks ago. He's wanted in Texas for murder. We'll report the death and see that his body's taken care of in Listow. What are you planning to do now?'

'We were talking about that just before we met up with you,' said Jack. 'We're pretty sure that Snyder was in Tresco just after we left there, and he must have got orders from Craig not long before that. If we backtrack Snyder's movements maybe we'll find out where Craig is. We'll go on to Listow with you now, and leave for Tresco at daybreak tomorrow.'

'Sorry we can't help you,' said Lawton. 'On the day after tomorrow we're mounting a big operation on the Texas border. But what I will do is deputize you and give you a badge, so that you have the law behind you while you're looking for Craig.'

9

When Jack and Ruth reached Tresco the following day they took two rooms at the hotel. Then Jack started making enquiries around town. The barkeep at the saloon was the most informative. He remembered Snyder from Jack's description, and said that he had given the stranger an account of the murder attempt at the hotel, and had told him that Jack and Ruth had left for Listow a few hours earlier, on the trail of the two men who had attempted to kill them. Further enquiries by Jack as to where Snyder had come from proved fruitless.

Jack returned to Ruth, and a little later they went to the hotel dining-room for a meal. They sat at a table next to one occupied by a man dressed in Eastern-style clothes. The man was a whiskey peddler from Arkansas. His name was Warren and he was riding through the territory promoting the sale of his company's wares.

Warren had just finished his meal. He took a large cigar from a box on the table and lit it. Glancing across at him, Jack noticed that the cigar-box was identical to the one carried by Snyder. He drew Ruth's attention to it, before rising and walking over to Warren's table.

'I'd be obliged,' he said, 'if you'd tell me where you got those cigars.' Warren smiled at him.

'I'm not surprised you're curious,' he said. 'They're very good cigars, and I buy them back home in Arkansas now and then when I can afford it. I've never seen them on sale in the territory, that is until yesterday. But you'll have to take a twenty-mile ride before you can buy any.'

'Where would that be?' asked Jack.

'At Parker's store, east of here,' Warren replied. 'It's a group of buildings standing alone in the middle of a big, flat stretch of ground. I called in yesterday for supplies and noticed the cigars on a shelf.'

Jack thanked Warren and returned to Ruth. He told her what he had just learnt. They decided to ride to Parker's store the following morning to see whether Snyder, and possibly Craig had called there recently.

As they approached the store the following morning they could see that it comprised a group of buildings which covered a large area. Jack pinned on his badge, then they dismounted and went inside the store. It was empty, save for Parker, who was sitting on a stool behind the counter attending to some paper work.

Parker looked up as they came in and immediately recognized them, from Craig's description, as the couple whom Snyder had been hired to kill. He concealed his alarm at their appearance at the store.

'Howdy folks,' he said. 'What can I do for you?'

Jack told him that he was looking for

two men. He described Snyder and Craig and asked Parker if he had seen either of them at the store recently.

'I'm pretty sure,' said Parker, 'that they ain't been here. What makes you think they might have called in?'

'The two men we're asking about are called Snyder and Craig,' said Jack. 'Snyder was hired by Craig to kill me and my partner here. Snyder's dead now, and in his belongings we found a box of cigars exactly the same as the one on the shelf behind you. And as far as we could find out, your store is the only place in this area where the cigars can be bought.'

'I have a man,' said Parker, 'who spells me off in the store now and again when I have other things to do. It could be that he served the man called Snyder. Wait here while I get him.'

As Parker rose to his feet, his leg knocked over the stool behind him.

'Darn it!' he said, and bent down behind the counter, ostensibly to pick up the stool. But when he rose to his feet he was holding a loaded shotgun with its hammer cocked. He pointed it at the couple in front of him.

'You know what this shotgun can do to you both,' he said. 'Let me see your hands up in the air as high as they'll go.'

Jack and Ruth had no option but to obey. Keeping them covered Parker opened one of the doors at the rear of the store and shouted to Pardoe, working outside the stable. He told him to bring Craig and his two men to the store.

When Craig saw the two prisoners his astonishment soon turned to grim satisfaction. Parker told him about Snyder's death, and the reason for the prisoners' call at the store.

'This *is* a stroke of luck,' said Craig. 'Apart from anything else, I won't have to pay Snyder the rest of his money.'

He turned to Parker. 'Where can we keep these two till we decide what to do with them?' he asked.

'There's a storeroom at the back of

the stable,' said Parker. 'They can go in there.'

Craig made no attempt to question the prisoners and they were taken to the stable, tied hand and foot, and left in the storeroom, with Pardoe on guard outside. In the store, which was empty of customers, Parker discussed the situation with Craig.

'I want those two out of here right now,' he said. 'Maybe there'll be more deputies coming along to join up with him.'

'You're right,' said Craig. 'We'll ride within the hour. Rooney and Vickery are both fit to ride now. We'll go to Saxon's place and get rid of Tracy on the way. We'll make his death look like an accident. We'll take the woman on with us. I reckon Saxon will pay a good price for her. You know what he's like with women.'

Fifty minutes later the six riders, including Pardoe, who was to help guard the prisoners, then report the death of Jack back to Parker, set off in a south-easterly direction. The prisoners' hands were tied. They camped out overnight, with a guard on the prisoners. After supper, lying on the ground with their hands and feet tied, Jack and Ruth heard snatches of conversation from the four men sitting by the fire. From these they gathered that the outlaws' destination was a place called Saxon Wells, not far from a town called Chantry.

At daybreak they continued their ride. Later in the morning they came to a flat-topped ridge running across their path. The slope to the top of the ridge was gentle at that point, and they rode slowly to the top, then turned and rode along it. After a while they came to a point where a gently sloping side gave way to a slope, stretching down from the flat top, of twelve feet or so, followed by a sheer drop of sixty feet to the ground below.

Here they stopped and they all dismounted except the prisoners. Craig and Pardoe, standing near Jack, with their backs to him, exchanged a few words which he could not hear. Then they suddenly turned, grabbed Jack's arm, and pulled him out of the saddle. As he hit the ground, Pardoe pistol-whipped him. Temporarily stunned, Jack lay motionless while Craig returned his victim's gun to its holster. Jack was still wearing his badge and his pockets had not been emptied. Pardoe cut the rope around Jack's wrists and removed it. Then he and Craig pushed Jack on to the slope and watched him slide down it.

As Jack reached the bottom of the slope he was falling almost feet first. The two watchers saw him grab and hold on to the edge at the top of the sheer face for a few moments. Then his grip gradually loosened and his hands disappeared from view. Any intervention by Ruth had been prevented by Vickery and Rooney, and she could only watch helplessly as Jack vanished from sight.

'We'll ride back to take a look at

Tracy,' said Craig, 'just to make sure he's dead. Then we'll be on our way.'

They were preparing to leave the scene when Pardoe drew Craig's attention to a group of riders in the far distance, moving in their direction. They all moved a little way down the slope on the other side of the ridge, then Pardoe and Craig crawled back to watch the approaching riders, who were still some way off.

'That sure looks like a posse to me,' said Craig. 'We'd better get out of here quick. Tracy *must* be dead. Nobody could be alive after a fall like that.'

They rode down the south side of the ridge and at the bottom parted company with Pardoe. He headed for Parker's store, while the rest of them continued in a south-easterly direction. Vickery led the horse on which Ruth was riding, distraught at the fate which had befallen Jack. She was under threat of being tied on her horse if she caused any trouble.

They bypassed Chantry and later in

the afternoon found themselves approaching Saxon Wells, a group of buildings in the centre of a large stretch of flat ground.

The buildings had been erected by a man called Saxon with the proceeds of criminal activities east of the Arkansas border. When things grew too hot for him there he moved into the Indian Territory. He chose a location for his enterprise, then dug two wells to supply the necessary water. These wells gave the place its name.

Following that, he built a hotel, gambling-hall, saloon providing girls and other entertainment, plus a store and livery stable. Ostensibly, the purpose of Saxon Wells was to provide food and entertainment for the weary traveller, as well as high-class accommodation. But most of Saxon's profits came from harbouring members of the criminal fraternity who, at the first indication of the arrival of an officer of the law, were whisked into an underground chamber with a concealed entrance. The cluster of buildings was surrounded by a tall barbed-wire fence, with only one gate in it, towards which Craig and the others were heading. On the top of one of the buildings was a platform for use as an observation post.

As Craig and the others reached the gate two armed men stepped out in front of them. From behind them a third man appeared. Craig recognized him as Parton, a short, bearded middle-aged man, who was Saxon's second in command.

'I reckon you remember me, Parton,' said Craig. 'I'd like a few words with Saxon.'

'He's gone to Arkansas,' said Parton. 'Should be back in five or six days. Meanwhile, I'm in charge here.'

'Can we stay here till he gets back?' asked Craig.

'Sure,' replied Parton, eyeing Ruth with some curiosity. 'We've got the room.'

Craig drew Parton aside and explained Ruth's presence.

'I brought her along,' he said, 'because I thought Saxon might be interested in meeting her.'

'I think you're right,' said Parton, well aware, as Craig was, of Saxon's abnormal sexual appetite. 'She sure is a good-looking woman. I'll keep her in Saxon's quarters till he gets back.'

'This spare horse we've got with us belonged to Tracy,' said Craig. 'Do what you want with it. And that applies to the woman's too.'

Craig and his two men were shown to rooms on the first floor of the hotel. Ruth was taken to a small bedroom in Saxon's quarters on the ground floor of the same building. There, she was bound hand and foot and laid on the bed, to which she was tied. She was warned that she would be gagged if she made any noise, and she was then left in the locked room. Alone in the room Ruth lay quiet, still badly shocked by Jack's murder, and dreading what the future might hold for her.

10

When Jack, stunned, was pushed down the slope from the top of the ridge by Craig and Pardoe, he came to just before he slid over the top of the sheer rock face below. Desperately, he held on to the edge with his fingers. He knew that he could only maintain this grip for a few seconds and he was sure that certain death awaited him below.

But when he *did* fall he only dropped a few inches before his feet landed on a narrow ledge and he realized that he had dropped into a shallow crevice on the rock-face. For a few moments he teetered on the balls of his feet, in danger of falling backwards into space. Then he leaned forward and rested against the rock-face. He could hear the faint sound of voices above for a short while. Then there was silence.

As he looked around him he could

see a number of footholds which should enable him to climb on to the slope above. He waited a further twenty minutes, leaning against the rock face. Then, slowly and carefully, he climbed up on to the slope above. He rested in a lying position for a while, then he slowly worked his way to the flat top of the ridge.

He looked around. There was nobody in sight. He felt the wound on his head. It was still bleeding slightly. He tied his bandanna around it, checked that his gun was loaded, and walked down the slope on the south side of the ridge. When he reached the bottom he struck out in a south-easterly direction. His head was still throbbing and he paused occasionally for a rest. As he trudged along the thought predominant in his mind was that, as speedily as possible, he must get to Saxon Wells and attempt to rescue Ruth.

He had covered about three miles when he saw a buggy converging on him from his right. It altered course, came straight towards him, and stopped. The man inside was slim, middle-aged, and neatly dressed. He looked Jack over, then spoke to him.

'I can see you're in trouble, Deputy,' he said. 'I'm Doc Sawyer from Chantry. Lucky for you I had a call to make out this way. I'll have a quick look at your head, then, if you want, you can tell me all about it while we're driving to town.'

Sawyer climbed out of the buggy and tended to Jack's wound. Then they both climbed in and started off towards Chantry.

'I'm guessing,' said Sawyer, 'that you were hit on the head with the barrel of a pistol.'

'That's right,' said Jack, and went on to tell the doctor about the events leading up to his injury. He asked Sawyer what he knew about the place called Saxon Wells.

'That's quite a story you've just told me,' said the doctor. 'Saxon Wells is south-east of Chantry, maybe fifteen miles. It was all built by a man called

Saxon who came from Arkansas. His idea, according to him, was to set up a place just for travellers passing through the territory — a place that would give them good food and accommodation, and plenty of entertainment.'

'Have you ever been there?' asked Jack.

'Only once,' Sawyer replied. 'Saxon had fallen off his horse and broken a leg. He called me in to set and splint it. He's a big, arrogant man, about fifty. If you're figuring on going there I can tell you that he has living-quarters in the hotel, the first building on the left inside the gate. The first door on the left inside the hotel leads to his quarters. And another thing, the group of buildings is circled by a tall barbed-wire fence, with only one gate in it, guarded by armed men. I didn't get a chance to see inside any of the other buildings. It was made pretty clear to me that it was time for me to leave.'

'It all sounds to me,' said Jack, 'as

though Saxon is harbouring criminals. It'll soon be dark. As soon as we reach Chantry I'll need a couple of horses — one of them for Ruth, a rifle and some supplies. Then I'll ride on to Saxon Wells. If I'm going to have any chance of rescuing Ruth, it must be done during the night.'

'My normal advice to anybody who's been hit as hard on the head as you were,' said Sawyer, 'would be for them to rest up for a while. The brain don't take kindly to a knock like that. But I can understand your worry about your partner. As for the things you want to pick up in Chantry, I'll get the horses for you and you can get a rifle at the store.'

'I want to send a telegraph message to the US marshal at Fort Smith,' said Jack. 'If I write it down can you hand it in for me?'

'Sure,' said Sawyer. 'Write it as soon as we reach Chantry, and maybe I can get it sent this evening.'

When they reached town Sawyer

took Jack into his house and gave him pencil and paper. The message written by Jack read:

SAXON WELLS SOUTH-EAST OF CHANTRY BEING USED BY SAXON TO HARBOUR CRIMINALS. CRAIG AND HIS MEN THERE WITH RUTH MAILER AS PRISONER. AM ATTEMPTING RESCUE HER. SEND HELP. CONTACT DOC SAWYER AT CHANTRY ON ARRIVAL. ADVISE THAT PARKERS STORE EAST OF TRESCO ALSO BEING USED TO HARBOUR CRIMINALS. JACK TRACY.

Jack handed the message over for the doctor to read. 'Can't say how long it'll be before they turn up here,' he said.

'I'll hand this in right now,' said Sawyer, 'then I'll come back, make you a meal and put a new bandage on. After that I'll get the two horses for you.'

'I'm mighty obliged for all this help you're giving me,' said Jack.

Later, when Sawyer had brought the horses, Jack took his leave of the doctor and walked the two horses over to the store. He bought a secondhand rifle, field glasses, a length of thin wire, wire cutters and some provisions. Then, leading the second horse, he rode off towards Saxon Wells.

It was a dark night, and he could see a few lights showing from the buildings and the gate well before he reached the place. He looked out for a grove of trees outside Saxon Wells, described to him by Sawyer, from which, in daylight, the entrance gate could be clearly seen. He led the horses to the centre of the grove and picketed them. He waited till midnight, then left the grove on foot and circled the buildings at a distance, before walking up to the fence at a point which was furthest from the gate. There were no lights on in the buildings close by.

He looked at the fence. As Sawyer had told him, it had been so designed as to be impossible to climb over in either direction. Using the cutters he severed three strands of barbed wire near the bottom and wormed his way through. Using the coil of thin wire he had brought with him, he joined together the ends of the barbed wire so that, in the dark, the cuts were invisible.

He moved cautiously along the fence towards the gate until he heard the faint sound of voices. He moved up to a rear corner of the hotel which was close to the fence. Peering round the corner, he could see the shadowy figures of the two guards at the gate. He listened to the conversation between them, then to their conversation with the two relief guards who turned up a little later. These conversations were extremely informative, as they related mainly to Ruth's arrival at Saxon Wells as a prisoner of Craig.

It seemed that Saxon was away, Ruth was being held in his quarters, and one of the relief guards had looked in on her only a few minutes before he arrived to take up his post.

Jack waited for a further twenty minutes after the guards who had been relieved left for the bunkhouse. Then he moved around the side wall of the hotel and along the front wall until he reached the entrance, which was not visible from the gate. Slowly, he opened the door and peered inside. The lobby was empty and a lighted oil-lamp was standing on the desk. He went in and closed the door behind him. On his left he saw the door leading to Saxon's private quarters. As he walked up to it he noticed that the key was in the lock. He unlocked the door and walked into a large living-room, luxuriously furnished. He closed the door behind him, then started to check the other doors leading out of the room. The first one he came to was locked. He turned the key and stepped inside.

The room was dimly lit by an oil-lamp standing on a table. On a bed on the far side of the room he saw Ruth. At first she did not recognize him. Then she stared at him in disbelief. She had been certain that he was dead. Jack ran up to the bed and cut through the ropes that were binding her.

'Are you all right, Ruth?' he asked. 'Did they harm you?'

Trembling a little, she shook her head, and Jack held her for a short while. Then he told her that they would escape through the fence to pick up two horses hidden in the grove.

Without incident they retraced Jack's steps to the place where he had cut the fence wires. He undid the ties holding them together and he and Ruth passed through. Carefully, he replaced the ties, then they started walking away from the fence to pick up the horses. They had only moved a few paces when Jack's legs gave way. He stumbled forward and collapsed on the ground. A moment later he sat up, shaking his head. Ruth knelt beside him.

'What's the matter, Jack?' she asked.

'Must be that knock I got on the head,' he said, rising to his feet. 'I'm all right now. Let's go.'

Just as they reached the horses in the middle of the grove, Jack turned to say something to Ruth, but in mid-sentence he suddenly collapsed on the ground and lay still. Ruth knelt down by him. His breathing seemed to be normal but she could not wake him. She laid him in a comfortable position and sat by his side, watching for the slightest sign of recovery, and considering what course of action she should take. Eventually, she decided that she had no option but to stay hidden in the grove until Jack came round, even though there was the risk of their being discovered.

★   ★   ★

In Saxon Wells, when the relief guard checked on Ruth just before four thirty in the morning, all hell broke loose. Parton called all the hands into the hotel and told them what had happened. He told two men to go round the fence and see if any wires had been cut. When they returned to report that the fence was intact, he told them to patrol it until further notice. Then he spoke to the rest of the hands.

'The woman had help from somebody,' he said, 'but it looks like she's still here. She's got to be found. Search the whole place and bring her to me when you find her.'

'What about the guests?' asked one of the hands.

'Search all their rooms,' said Parton. 'Tell them it's an emergency.' But an intensive search lasting over an hour produced no sign of Ruth, and an increasingly worried Parton ordered a detailed inspection of the fence with the aid of lamps. Fifteen minutes later he was told that three wires had, in fact, been cut.

He realized now that the woman and her rescuer could have left Saxon Wells as much as five and a half hours earlier, in a direction unknown to him. It would be pointless to send out men to search for them. The situation was critical, since a visit by law officers in the near future was inevitable. He ordered a hand to visit the rooms of all the guests and ask them to come to the dining-room as a matter of urgency.

When they had assembled Parton told them that it appeared now that the woman prisoner had left Saxon Wells with her rescuer, probably a few hours ago, and a visit by the law could be expected soon. He suggested they should all leave after breakfast, which would be served in twenty minutes.

As the guests left to return to their rooms, Parton flushed as he heard Craig's parting remark. 'It's a pity they didn't keep a better watch on the woman.'

Dawn broke during breakfast, and soon after this the guests started to leave, riding off in various directions. When they had all departed, Parton, whose intention was to advise Saxon in Arkansas as soon as possible of events at Saxon Wells, also left. He was accompanied by all the hands Saxon had brought with him from Arkansas to establish Saxon Wells. The only people left behind were the saloon-girls and those employed on cleaning duties and other menial tasks.

*　*　*

Half an hour after dawn, Jack was still lying motionless, with Ruth by his side. She rose to her feet, picked up the field glasses, and walked to the edge of the grove. Looking towards Saxon Wells, she could see no guards at the gate, but there appeared to be a lot of activity inside the fence. As she watched, riders started to emerge through the gate in small groups until she had counted a total of fifteen riders. One of the groups she was able to identify as Craig accompanied by Vickery and Rooney. After passing through the gate these three riders swung round and headed west.

She went to look at Jack. He had not moved. She returned to watch the activity at Saxon Wells and it was not long before she saw another bunch of riders leaving, totalling about twelve. She identified Parton in the lead. The group of riders moved towards the south-east. Ruth waited for a while, but no further riders appeared, and she could see people still moving around inside the fence.

She went back to Jack and sat beside him, worried by the fact that he still showed no sign of coming to. The day passed slowly, and occasionally she went to look through the glasses at Saxon Wells. She was sitting beside Jack just before nightfall, when he suddenly stirred, then sat up and looked at Ruth.

'What's happened, Ruth?' he asked. 'The last thing I remember is walking up to the horses here, in the dark.'

Ruth told him about his collapse, and about what she had seen through the glasses earlier in the day.

'How d'you feel now, Jack?' she asked. 'I've been scared half to death.'

'The headache's gone,' Jack replied,

'and it's a long time since I've been as hungry as I am right now.'

'Same here,' said Ruth. 'Let's use up some of those provisions you brought with you.'

Over the meal they discussed their next move. Jack said that it looked as though, because of Ruth's escape and the certainty that the law would be arriving soon, all the criminals had left, followed by Parton and his men. It was unlikely that anyone left there would present any danger to them. They decided to take some rest and ride over to Saxon Wells in the morning.

Next day, when Jack and Ruth rode through the gate, there was no one visible outside the buildings. They dismounted and went into the hotel. They heard the faint sound of voices behind one of the doors. Jack opened it and he and Ruth stepped inside the large well-furnished dining-room. Near the end of a long polished dining-table six saloon-girls were sitting, taking a meal. A somewhat older woman was sitting at the head of the table. They all stared at the man with the badge and his companion.

'Hello, folks,' said the older woman. 'I'm Lucy Rainbow and these are my girls. What can we do for you?'

'I suppose you know,' said Jack, 'that you've been entertaining criminals?'

'Of course we do,' said Lucy. 'We ain't fools. We were hired in Amarillo and it wasn't till we got here that we found out who our clients were going to be. And Saxon wouldn't let us leave. Now we're stuck here. Can you help us to get out?'

'Just now,' said Jack, 'I'm on the trail of three of the men who left here. I have to leave. But there'll be some more deputies turning up pretty soon. They'll help you. If I give you a letter for them, will you hand it over?'

'Sure,' said Lucy, 'and meanwhile we're enjoying the high-class food and comfort that Saxon handed out to his guests.'

Jack wrote a letter saying that he and

Ruth were following Craig and his two men, who had headed west on leaving Saxon Wells. He handed the letter to Lucy, then he and Ruth rode to the point where Craig and his companions had disappeared from Ruth's view. Here they found some recently made horse-tracks, probably made by the riders they were following. The tracks were on a trail leading due west.

They followed the trail, catching sight of the tracks from time to time, until late afternoon, when they came upon a dead horse, still saddled, lying a little way off the trail. It had been shot through the head. The horse's leg was broken and there were signs that it had stepped into a hole nearby. They rode on until darkness fell, then made camp.

In the morning, after riding for an hour, Jack realized it was a while since he had seen the tracks they had been following. As he turned to speak to Ruth, they heard the sounds of three rifle shots, equally spaced, coming from the left. Looking in that direction, they saw smoke on the side of a ridge. Using the glasses, Jack could see a man sitting near the smoke, waving his arms. He handed the glasses to Ruth.

'Somebody in trouble over there,' he said. 'Let's go and see.'

They rode up the side of the ridge to a man who was sitting close to a patch of brush not far from the top of the slope. The man was elderly, bearded, and roughly dressed. His face was deeply tanned by long hours spent in the open.

'I sure am glad to see you folks,' he said. 'I've got me a busted leg. Tripped at the top of the slope there in the dark, and fell on it. I've been here for two nights. The name's Tomlin, by the way, Hank Tomlin.'

Jack introduced himself and Ruth, then examined the leg, between the knee and ankle.

'It's a break,' he said, 'and not a clean one. You've got to see a doctor. Where's the nearest one?'

'At Carlin,' Tomlin replied. 'That's

about sixteen miles west of here.'

'First we need splints for your leg,' said Jack.'

'I live in a shack just on the other side of the ridge,' said Tomlin. 'There's plenty of bits of timber there.'

Jack and Ruth tied Tomlin's legs together and hoisted him over the back of Ruth's horse. Then they made their way over the top of the ridge to Tomlin's shack, where Jack made a couple of splints and tied them in place. When this had been done, Jack spoke to Tomlin, while Ruth prepared some food for the old man.

'The only way to get you to Carlin without damaging that leg any more is by travois,' he said. 'I see some small trees over there. I'll bring some timber back from there and build one in no time.'

While he was building the travois Jack asked Tomlin why he had been on the far side of the ridge after dark. Tomlin explained that two days ago, in the evening, three men, two on one horse, had ridden up to the shack and he had noticed them showing some interest in his horse which was picketed close by. The men had said that they would camp there for the night, and they built a camp-fire a little way from the shack and sat by it eating their supper.

Both Jack and Ruth pricked up their ears at the mention of the three men, and Jack asked Tomlin to describe them. The descriptions given left no doubt that the three were Craig and his men. Jack told Tomlin that the men were the ones that he and Ruth were following, and he asked him what had happened next.

'I didn't feel easy about those three,' said Tomlin, 'so as soon as it was really dark I snuck up behind a boulder close to them and listened to them talking. It was a while before I was mentioned. But when I was, it was clear that I was going to be killed before they left, and they were going to take my horse. So I got my rifle from the shack and walked across the ridge with the idea of hiding in that patch of brush you found me sitting by. After the fall I only just managed to crawl into it, and then out of it later when I figured they'd left.'

'I sure wish we knew where those three were heading when they left here,' said Jack.

'Maybe I can help you there,' said Tomlin. 'Before they mentioned me they had a long talk about an operation that they were planning. It seems that they were running short of money and the plan was to kidnap for ransom the wife of a cattleman called Redford somewhere in the Texas Panhandle.'

'I've heard of him,' said Jack. 'He owns the Box R. It's a big spread in the south of the Panhandle. You could call him one of the cattle barons. Did you hear just how they were going to carry out this kidnap?'

'No,' replied Tomlin. 'That's all I can tell you, except that the telegraph operator in a place called Amity close to the ranch will be feeding them information about the Redfords. Oh, and one other thing. They're expecting to pick up two more men in the Panhandle to help them in the operation.'

'The information you just gave us,' said Jack, 'is going to help us a lot. When we've handed you over to the doctor in Carlin we'll ride straight to the Box R to warn Redford. Then we'll go to see US Marshal Dixon in Amarillo, and settle on a plan to capture Craig and the others.'

As Jack continued his work on the travois Ruth spoke to the injured man.

'I've been wondering, Mr Tomlin,' she said. 'Why do you live alone here?'

'Until a year ago, when I had to give it up,' said Tomlin, 'I'd been a wandering prospector for twenty years, always working on my own. I tried settling down in Carlin, but I couldn't stand having all those people around. That's why I came here. But after what's just happened here, maybe I'll give Carlin another go. The doctor'll help me. He's a good friend of mine.'

The travois was finished soon after and they headed for Carlin, Ruth riding double with Jack. They arrived there in the evening and handed Tomlin over to his friend the doctor. Jack and Ruth spent the night at the hotel and early the following morning they set off on the long ride to the Box R.

11

When Jack and Ruth arrived at the Box R and saw the size of the buildings, it was an indication to them of how big the ranch was. As they approached the big house a man came out of one of the other buildings and intercepted them. He asked them their business.

'We'd like to see Mr Redford,' said Jack, 'on a private and very urgent matter.'

Jake Yardley, the foreman, hesitated for a moment, then told them to wait. A few minutes later, Redford came out with Yardley and walked up to them. The rancher was a stocky, bearded, well-dressed man in his early fifties. His face gave a hint of the determination which had brought him from cowboy to cattle baron.

Jack introduced Ruth and himself.

'I remember those names,' said

Redford. 'My friend Marshal Dixon in Amarillo was talking about you when I was there a few days ago. He said you two were chasing the Laredo gang through the Indian Territory. So I'm curious to know why you're here.'

'The gang is planning to kidnap your wife,' said Jack.

Alarmed, Redford invited Jack and Ruth into the house and beckoned to Yardley to follow. They joined Lois Redford in the living-room. She was a handsome raven-haired woman, a few years younger than her husband. Jack passed on everything that Tomlin had told him.

'We're on our way to see Marshal Dixon in Amarillo,' he said, 'to set up a plan to catch the gang, but we've come here first, to warn you that Mrs Redford needs to be guarded until the gang is captured. When we've seen the marshal we'll be coming back here to tell you about the plan we've worked out.'

'We're mighty obliged for the warning,' said the rancher. 'We'll see to it that my wife's kept out of danger.'

'It would help us,' said Jack, 'if nobody here, outside the people in this room, knows about the kidnap threat and the plan to capture the gang.'

'Understood,' said the rancher. 'I'm surprised to hear that Ford the telegraph operator in Amity is in cahoots with the gang. Maybe we should keep an eye on him. His office is next to the livery stable and that's run by Andy Trent. Andy helped me build up the Box R. I'd trust him with my life. He'll keep an eye on Ford if I ask him.'

'That's a good idea,' said Jack.

'Right,' said Redford. 'You stay here and have a meal with us while Jake rides in to Amity to ask Andy to help us out and tell us if he's noticed anything different about Ford's behaviour lately.'

When the foreman returned he had some interesting news. Two days earlier, in the evening, Andy had noticed a horse standing outside Ford's house behind the telegraph office. And on the following evening Ford had hired a horse from the liveryman for three hours, saying he felt like some exercise and fresh air after a day in the office.

'It looks like the gang's already here,' said Jack. 'We'd best be on our way. We'll be back here as soon as things are organized.'

They took their leave of the Redfords and their foreman and bypassing Amity, they rode to Amarillo. It was late in the evening when they arrived and they decided to wait until morning before seeing Marshal Dixon. They took two rooms at the hotel.

Dixon was in his office when Ruth and Jack called round after breakfast. Surprised to see Jack, he stood up as they approached the desk.

'Jack!' he said. 'I thought you were in the Indian Territory.'

Jack introduced Ruth.

'I've heard a lot about you, Miss Mailer,' said the marshal, 'and it's clear that Craig will rue the day that he shot your father.'

'It's something I have to do,' she said.

Jack gave Dixon a full account of the pursuit of Craig and his men through the Indian Territory, and of the recent call at the Box R. He said that he and Ruth had thought up a plan for capturing the gang which needed the marshal's help, and they would like his opinion of it. He proceeded to explain the plan in detail.

'I like it,' said Dixon, when Jack had finished. 'I can get help from the Texas Rangers. I can arrange with the stagecoach line for an empty north-bound coach to turn up at Amity at the scheduled time on the day in question. As for the telegraph message you're going to send from the Box R to Amarillo about Redford's wife travelling there on the stage, it could be sent to her sister who lives here. She'll pass it to me.'

'We're riding back to the Box R now,' said Jack. 'We'll send the telegraph message before the office in Amity closes today. Now today's Tuesday. If

197

the message says that Mrs Redford is travelling on the noon stage on Thursday, does that give you enough time to organize things?'

'It's enough,' said Dixon, 'and I'm hoping we can put the Laredo gang out of action once and for all. I haven't forgotten the number of lawmen they've killed.'

'Will you get the rangers to ride into Amity about twenty minutes before the stage is due, and not earlier?' asked Jack. 'That's what Ruth and I will do.'

'I'll see to that,' said the marshal, 'and before you go I'm going to appoint you both deputy US marshals for this operation.'

Jack and Ruth rode back to the Box R, bypassing Amity on the way. They told Redford and his wife of the proposed plan of action. Then, with their help they wrote a telegraph message to Mrs Redford's sister in Amarillo saying that Mrs Redford would travel alone on the noon stage on Thursday to stay with her sister for a couple of days to do some shopping.

The foreman took the message to the telegraph office and handed it to Ford. Then, leaving his horse at the hitching-rail outside the saloon, he walked back to the livery stable. Trent showed him into his house behind the stable, then returned to his work. An hour and a half later he returned to tell the foreman that Ford had just hired a horse and ridden out of town. Yardley took the news back to the ranch.

'Looks like he's taken the bait,' said Jack. 'Now all we have to do is wait until we and the rangers board the stagecoach at Amity on Thursday.

'We hope you'll stay here with us,' said Lois Redford. 'I'd welcome some female company.' She smiled at her husband. 'I get pretty tired of listening to folk talking about cows all the time. And we've already told the hands that you two are relatives of mine on a short visit.'

And so it was agreed.

★　★　★

In a ravine located a little way off the main trail running between Amity and Amarillo, and a little over twenty miles north of Amity, Craig was sitting by a camp-fire. With him were Rooney and the two new members of the gang. These were Hix and Verity, old acquaintances of Craig, who had recently left the state penitentiary after serving terms for armed robbery.

The four men stiffened as they heard the sound of a horse approaching them in the darkness. Their hands moved to the handles of their sixguns. They relaxed as Vickery hailed them. He fastened his horse to the picket line, then walked up to the fire.

'It's good news,' he said. 'Ford was waiting at the meeting place when I got there. He'd just sent a telegraph message from Redford's wife to her sister in Amarillo saying she would be travelling alone to Amarillo to see her. She said she would be travelling on the noon stage from Amity on Thursday, the day after tomorrow.'

'That really *is* good news,' said Craig. 'It makes our job a lot easier. We've held up plenty of stage-coaches in our time.'

'Ford says he knows the stagecoach route well,' said Vickery, 'and he says there's one spot that's just right for us to hide in while we're waiting for the coach. It's a gully, just a little way off the route and about six miles north of the first swing station from Amity.'

'I'll take a look at it in the morning,' said Craig.

★　★　★

On Thursday morning, twenty minutes before noon, Jack and Ruth met three rangers in Amity at the boarding point for the stagecoach. The Ranger in charge was Fallon. He told Jack that Dixon had wanted more Rangers to be sent, but no more could be spared.

'So it's five against five,' said Jack.

'But we have the big advantage of surprise.'

Fallon told Jack that the passengers in the stage-coach had been taken off at the first home station south of Amity, and a relief coach would pick them up there later. Then they discussed the details of the operation.

Ford, working in his office, heard the stage roll in a little before noon. He walked over to the window and looked along the street. The coach had come to a halt. Standing against it were three Rangers and a man and a woman. The woman was *not* Lois Redford. While the horses were being changed, one Ranger climbed on to the driver's box and the other four people standing there climbed inside the coach.

Ford's jaw dropped, and he panicked. His first thought was to get word to the gang to abort the operation. He should be able to get to them in time. Hastily, he printed a notice on a card. It read: TELEGRAPH LINE DOWN. BACK LATER. He hung the card on the outside of his office door and ran to the livery stable. Inside the door he stopped short as Yardley and Trent confronted him. The foreman had a pistol in his hand.

'You can drop the idea,' said Yardley, 'of riding to warn Craig. We're holding you here till the Rangers get back.'

The stagecoach headed for the first swing station north of Amity, twelve miles distant. The Ranger on the box was Avery, who had past experience of driving a six-horse team. They reached the first swing station without incident, and two stock-tenders changed the horses. They had seen no suspicious characters around. After driving the stage a further six miles, Avery shouted down to the others that he had spotted a movement in a gully off to the left.

Moments later, as the coach drew abreast of the gully, five riders came out of it and headed in a direction that would bring them up to the coach from behind. Each of them was holding a sixgun in his hand. They started firing these into the air, and the driver slowed down the horses. As the stagecoach came to a halt, he raised both arms in the air. He was wearing nothing to indicate he was a lawman.

The gang divided as they approached the coach from behind. Craig and Hix approached the right hand side, the other three the left. Inside the coach, Ruth and Fallon were ready to open fire on the right hand side, Jack and the other Ranger on the left.

As soon as the oncoming riders were within range, they were met by a fusillade from the coach, to which Avery, who had stepped off the driver's box to shelter behind it, made his own contribution. Four of the riders fell from their horses. Craig, hit by a shot from Ruth which grazed the side of his head, slumped forward, but did not fall from the saddle.

The occupants of the coach spilled out and each one ran towards a member of the gang to disarm him. Ruth ran towards Craig, but as she drew near he straightened up and they fired simultaneously at each other. Hit in the leg, Ruth collapsed on the ground. Although hit in the shoulder, Craig managed to turn his horse and ride off to the north before anyone could stop him.

Of the four men on the ground, Rooney and Vickery were dead. The other two had been hit in the chest, but would probably survive. Jack ran round the coach and up to Ruth. A bullet had torn the flesh on the side of her leg, just above the knee, before passing on. Jack got the first-aid box from the coach and cleaned and bandaged the wound.

Just as Jack finished, Fallon came up to them to see how Ruth was.

He told them that Avery would drive the coach back to Amity with Ruth and Jack inside, and the two wounded prisoners on top. The two dead men could be collected later. He himself, and the other Ranger, would go in search of the wounded Craig, riding two of the horses used by the gang.

When the coach reached Amity it stopped outside the doctor's house, and Jack carried Ruth inside. The Box R foreman, who happened to be in town, saw this, and Avery told him what had happened. Inside his house Doc Hanley examined the wound on Ruth's leg.

'You're lucky,' he said. 'An inch to one side and it could have caused a lot more damage. As it is, it should heal up without leaving too much of a scar. But you've got to rest up for a while. I'll clean it up and put a bandage on. Then I'll have a look at those two men outside. I'll see you again soon.'

They thanked the doctor and Jack carried Ruth to the hotel, where they took two rooms. But an hour later, Lois Redford came into town driving a two-seat buggy, and insisted that Ruth and Jack stayed at the Box R until Ruth was fit.

Two days later, Hanley came out to the ranch in the morning to see Ruth. He said the wound was healing up well, with no sign of complications. In the afternoon, Fallon called at the ranch to let Jack and Ruth know that the search for Craig had been unsuccessful. He said that he and his partner had combed a large area without finding any sign of him and nobody had reported sighting him.

'We can't spend any more time here,' he said. 'We'll have to be satisfied with what we've done. But I guess you two won't rest till Craig's found.'

When Fallon had left, Jack told Ruth that he intended to leave the following morning for the place where Craig had been wounded, in an effort to pick up his trail before it was too late.

'You know,' said Ruth, 'how much I wish I was coming along with you.'

'I know,' said Jack. 'I wish the same thing myself. But one way you can help is by telling me about Craig's horse. I think you got a good look at it.'

'Yes I did,' said Ruth. 'It was a good-looking horse — a big chestnut with a white blaze down its face.'

12

When Jack left the Box R the following morning at daybreak, he first rode to the scene of the hold-up, from which the injured Craig had been seen riding to the north towards the next swing station, six miles away. Jack headed in that direction, and after riding three miles he left the trail to investigate a rough area of terrain on his left. He found no sign of Craig there, and decided to visit the swing station. When it came in view he could see that he was approaching it from the rear.

As he drew close he could hear sounds coming from the stable, whose rear door was open. He dismounted and walked inside. Startled, Lonnigan and his wife, who were cleaning out the stable, stared at the man with the badge. Both in their thirties, they were running the swing station, and their boy

Johnny, aged ten, was living there with them. Jack looked round the stable before he spoke. He noted the look of deep apprehension on the faces of the couple facing him.

'Howdy,' he said. 'I'm looking for one of the men who held up the stage two days ago. I called to see if you'd seen anything of him. But before you answer, I think you have.'

He pointed to a horse in a stall on his right. It looked out of place among the others. It was a big chestnut with a white blaze down its face.

'I'm sure that's the horse belonging to Craig, the man I'm after,' said Jack.

Distraught, the couple walked up to Jack.

'For God's sake!' said Lonnigan. 'He's in a bedroom at the front of the house with our boy Johnny. He's only ten. Craig's threatened to shoot him through the head if we tell anybody he's here.'

They went on to tell Jack how Craig had arrived two days ago and had forced Lonnigan to take a bullet out of his left shoulder and treat the wound. To ensure his own safety, the outlaw had taken Lonnigan's weapons into the bedroom, and had locked himself in there with the boy for the last two nights. During the day he had insisted that either the boy or his mother must be in the bedroom with him at any time, with the door closed.

'We're lucky you came in the back way,' Lonnigan said, 'otherwise Craig would have seen you.'

At Jack's request, the Lonnigans described the interior of the room where Craig was holding the boy, and they showed him the interior of the house.

'I have a plan,' said Jack, 'that might be a little dangerous for you, Mrs Lonnigan, but maybe you'd be willing to take the risk. When can you go into the room to let Johnny come out for a spell while you stay in there?'

'I can do that now,' she said. 'I'll say there's some food waiting for Johnny in the kitchen.'

Jack described his plan to them and they both agreed. Five minutes later Grace Lonnigan knocked on the door of the room where Craig was sitting up in bed, his back resting against two pillows. A cocked and loaded sixgun rested on the bed close to his right hand. He called out to Grace to come in. She opened the door, went inside the room, and a minute later Johnny came out, closed the door behind him, and went into the kitchen where his father and Jack explained to him his part in the plan.

Five minutes later, Jack stood outside the door of Craig's room, holding his sixgun; Lonnigan was standing outside the house, against the wall by the side of the window of Craig's room; and Johnny was standing in the doorway leading into the house, from which position he could see both his father and Jack.

At a sign from Jack, Johnny signalled his father, who lifted the heavy sledge-hammer he was holding and swung it against the centre of the window of Craig's room. Jack pushed the door open and stepped into the doorway. Simultaneously Grace Lonnigan dropped from the chair she was sitting on and lay on the floor at the foot of the bed. As the window shattered and pieces of glass fell on the bed Craig picked up his gun and looked towards the window. Seeing nobody there, he turned quickly and saw Jack in the doorway. He recognized him instantly.

Craig was bringing his gun round to bear on his opponent when a bullet from Jack's Peacemaker drilled into his heart and he slumped sideways on the bed. Jack checked that he was dead, then helped Grace Lonnigan to her feet as Lonnigan and Johnny came into the room.

'It's all over,' said Jack, 'both for you *and* me.'

Jack helped Lonnigan carry Craig's body into a storeroom in the stable. He said he would arrange for the undertaker in Amity to collect it. Then he left for Amity where he went to the telegraph office, staffed by a new operator, and sent a message to Marshal Dixon, advising him of Craig's death, and saying that he himself would be staying at the Box R until Ruth was fit to travel. Then he rode to the ranch.

Quickly, he told the Redfords what had happened. Then he went to Ruth's room. She smiled, greatly relieved to see him.

'Our job's done, Ruth,' he said, and told her what had happened.

'You know, Ruth,' he said, 'that I have a ranch in Colorado. On the way back here I've been wondering what you'd think of the idea of helping me to run it.'

'Does this mean,' Ruth smiled, 'that you're figuring to make an honest woman of me?'

'If you'll have me,' Jack replied. 'A future without you don't appeal to me one little bit.'

'That's exactly the way I feel,' said Ruth, 'so the answer to your question is 'Yes'.'

The Redfords insisted that they be married on the Box R, and three days after the ceremony they headed for the Box T in Colorado. There they embarked on a happy and contented life running a successful cattle ranch and raising a family.

And every now and then, particularly when they happened to hear the mournful strains of 'The Streets of Laredo', memories came flooding back of their long and perilous pursuit of the infamous Laredo gang.

THE END

We do hope that you have enjoyed reading this large print book.

Did you know that all of our titles are available for purchase?

We publish a wide range of high quality large print books including:
Romances, Mysteries, Classics
General Fiction
Non Fiction and Westerns

Special interest titles available in large print are:
The Little Oxford Dictionary
Music Book, Song Book
Hymn Book, Service Book

Also available from us courtesy of Oxford University Press:
Young Readers' Dictionary
(large print edition)
Young Readers' Thesaurus
(large print edition)

For further information or a free brochure, please contact us at:
Ulverscroft Large Print Books Ltd.,
The Green, Bradgate Road, Anstey,
Leicester, LE7 7FU, England.
Tel: (00 44) **0116 236 4325**
Fax: (00 44) **0116 234 0205**

SATAN'S GUN

Bill Williams

Nineteen-year-old Sam Bryson faces a conflict that will test his courage, character and faith. Raised mostly by his grandparents, Sam was made to practise with his pistol every day, except Sunday. Yet Albert Bryson's beloved wife had raised Sam to reject violence. Bryson orders Sam and his cousin, Jack, to hunt down his ranch hand's murderer, Sharkey Kelsall. Sam Bryson has no desire to kill, but soon discovers that when his own life is threatened he must protect himself.

BLUECOAT RENEGADE

Dale Graham

Lieutenant Chadwick Stanton is based at Fort Leavenworth in Kansas. His over-extravagant lifestyle causes him to initiate a robbery of the regimental payroll, but blame is placed squarely on his envied and hated rival, fellow officer, Captain Bentley Wallace. The trial, a foregone conclusion, results in the shamed officer being drummed out of the service. Now Ben wants retribution. But Stanton, in a cataclysmic showdown in a remote Wyoming canyon, is determined to thwart him. Can Ben find justice?

HARD MEN RIDING

Elliot Conway

Texan man Raynor, and his Mexican compadre Santos, had once been in Jake Petch's gang of bank robbers. After a raid in Grantsburg, Petch had bushwhacked Raynor and Santos, left them for dead and taken all the gold. Two years later, Raynor learns that Petch is now a big rancher in Arizona, and sets out with Santos on the vengeance trail. They leave a long tally of dead men before they finally face Petch. Can they settle the score?